About the Author

The author has been writing most of his life, mainly short horror stories. In the '70s some were broadcast on the old Capital Radio, and also on a popular radio station in Israel. Strange to tell, his first two published books (through AUSTIN MACAULEY) were Medico Science Faction (about the world's first attempt at a living, human brain transplant), and a children's story about a dog called 'GEORGE'. This is his fourth book.

To:

HUW JEFFREY
He who has kept my various laptops, printers and the like functioning, as well as providing encouragement and friendship over many years.

William P. Thomson

INSANITUS 2

AUSTIN MACAULEY PUBLISHERS™
LONDON · CAMBRIDGE · NEW YORK · SHARJAH

Copyright © William P. Thomson (2020)

The right of William P. Thomson to be identified as author of this work has been asserted by the author in accordance with section 77 and 78 of the Copyright, Designs and Patents Act 1988.

All rights reserved. No part of this publication may be reproduced, stored in a retrieval system, or transmitted in any form or by any means, electronic, mechanical, photocopying, recording, or otherwise, without the prior permission of the publishers.

Any person who commits any unauthorized act in relation to this publication may be liable to criminal prosecution and civil claims for damages.

This is a work of fiction. Names, characters, businesses, places, events, locales, and incidents are either the products of the author's imagination or used in a fictitious manner. Any resemblance to actual persons, living or dead, or actual events is purely coincidental.

A CIP catalogue record for this title is available from the British Library.

ISBN 9781528999083 (Paperback)
ISBN 9781528999090 (ePub e-book)

www.austinmacauley.com

First Published (2020)
Austin Macauley Publishers Ltd
25 Canada Square
Canary Wharf
London
E14 5LQ

Table Of Contents

The Decimation of Dingle Dickinson 9

Blow 28

Bogey 32

Stuffed! 35

Imagination's Child 38

'Charlie Mumbles' 42

Whyte 50

Fire! 55

The Decimation of Dingle Dickinson
(Or the Bogeyman!)

I

Dingle Dickinson cursed his parent's weird humour, from the moment he was of age and mind enough to grasp the full stupidity of his absurd Christian name: DINGLE.

Dingle! Think upon that name. Let it move about your mind and tongue. Savour the banality of it. **DINGLE!**

It did not end there. Had Dickinson been a little weed of a man, perhaps. But, he wasn't. He stood six feet six in his socks and of weight enough and more.

One can suppose that there is a blessing in most things, and size was certainly Dingle's. All sane people thought twice before making any sort of comment about his Christian name, the more so in the knowledge as to the body to which it was attached. Of course, the occasional fool, usually filled with too much booze, did make jolly with the name and, as a consequence, frequented a hospital ward for a period of time. Mostly, people simply called the man Dick, as he invited them to do, it being the first part of his surname and, of itself, an abbreviation for Richard, and which he preferred over Dingle; no contest, really! Sometimes, just to be on the safe side, most so permitted, played safe and called him Richard!

In spite of being lumbered by such a name, Dickinson made out well in life. Although rather on the rough side, he had both looks and brain. He met, and eventually married, a young local beauty with the simple, but oft incorrectly spelt name of Jayne: as you'll note, hers being with a 'y'.

In the course of time, they were blessed with a beautiful child. A girl. Here, at the naming, came the first indication as to Dingle Dickinson's attitude to his daughter. Whilst Jayne had set her heart on naming their little treasure Sarah Jayne – with a 'y' – Dickinson, it was destined not to be. Between that intention and the christening, Dingle got in and nailed his daughter with the Christian names of Clara Bo.

Now, it is possible to make that not altogether common female set of names charming, in their way, in the speaking of. To apply the correct nuances to same.

It was in this single regard, that Dingle's true act of cruelty was to be seen and heard.

Each syllable was a tiny spit of vengeance against his parents and *that* name. The nuances *he* applied to his daughter's Christian names turned them into something that sounded like a curse from the lips of Hell, rather than the soft, sweet sounds from Heaven's lips. Jayne insisted on calling her little treasure "Claire", and spelling it so.

Obviously, it would be some time before Clara (aka "Claire") Bo would be fully aware of, though not understand, her loving father's actions, and even the wife tried to persuade herself that it was her imagination that the names had been given in an act of spite. That her beloved husband had chosen them with love and good intent, and always spoken them in the same spirit.

Clara Bo – sans the 'w'. It had a certain ring to it, not to mention that it had once been the name of a famous film star from a golden age long since departed. Anyway, that's how Dingle always explained his choice to his wife and friends when so pressed to do. Mind you, when he used the term 'a certain ring about them' (the names, that is), he always did so with his face hidden from view, as if he were hiding a very secret, malicious grin; which he invariably was.

The years went by. Clara Bo Dickinson grew into yet another sort of horrendous Shirley Temple look-alike, even though her name was all wrong. You know the type, the one that mothers doth love, whilst all sane, rational and objective souls doth loathe!

As for Dingle Dickinson, he was just husband and father. Went to work, made money and kept himself to himself. He paid only minimal attention to his daughter. He didn't really love her as such, truth to tell. Perhaps she just brought back memories of his big, loathsome sister, Penelope, who had treated him with scant regard, when she wasn't thwacking him with her dollies those many years past.

It should be pointed out that the passing of time did nothing for the manner in which father continued to speak daughter's name: Clara alone, sometimes with the Bo bit to boot, and with great emphasis. Other times, with all the cruelty of nuance he could muster. Mind you, never when his wife was within earshot. He was sneaky like that. Interesting to note, the object of the verbal abuse did not respond in any negative way. Quite the opposite. She was full of sickly , gooey displays of love, affection and delight towards daddy.

We move on.

Jayne Dickinson, the mother, as you'll recall, was a full-time housewife, who busied herself in a multiple of things. Her life was full, active, constructive and blessed. Blessed by the presence of her very own, beloved little "Shirley Temple". Claire, as mother most often called her. No wonder the little mite was so confused.

Now then, as you will be aware, this is a sad little story being told, not to mention weird, although that later aspect shall remain in the shadows, for now.

The sad element, however, now commences. Let's say another year forward in the Dickinson household, and the obnoxious traits of mother's little darling were beginning to blossom, seeming to be much emphasized in the mind and eye of her father.

It must be made clear that in basic matters such as good manners, grace and discipline, mummy's little blessing could not be faulted, for which both parents were much grateful. However, as can be guessed, the situation did not remain so.

The road to sadness, tragedy and weirdness began, of all things, with a laugh. Let us be exact here. A child's laugh. Clara Bo's laugh, when she heard – and appreciated for the first time – her father's Christian name, which, as you'll remember, just happened to be DINGLE!

I shall not dwell on the details as to how the revelation came to little Clara, but simply state that as a result of that particular indiscretion by the man who had made clear the stupidity of the name, there were more redundant teeth about the room than might be found in a host of dental surgeries, and the unfortunate sucked up food through a straw for many a week!

After the revelation, daughter and father began to use their terrible respective Christian names against one another, as combatants might use weapons. Obviously, the little girl, so tender of years, was no match for her father, so it was all rather one-sided. Perhaps it was this alone that made her decide, in her ever-growing, mother-nourished, devious little mind, to employ a time-honoured direct method of attack and revenge. Namely, giving full vent to the power of her little lungs during the late hours of night, and the infant hours of each new day, with little pause betwixt the two.

Dingle Dickinson's answer to this sudden tactical change in the warfare was not of his thinking, but one of his colleagues. The bringing into play of a very special ancient of days, and the curse of the night to every child: the **BOGEYMAN**.

Dingle Dickinson pondered his colleague's suggestion. In truth, he didn't really have the imagination to expand the genesis of the idea, so his colleague spelt it out for him.

Now, imagine if you will, two grown up men of the world, in the midst of their work, in a profession itself testament to the technology of the modern age, speaking of something best left to the undisciplined, fevered imaginations of the very young – or insane: the **BOGEYMAN!!**

'It's simple, really, Dick. You just tell her that if she doesn't go to sleep, the bogeyman would come and snatch her away.'

'Just that?,' questioned Dingle Dickinson, not believing any miracle could be so simple and effective.

'Well, you can embellish it a bit if needs be,' suggested the colleague helpfully.

So, the seed was sown, the growing of the diabolical plot immediate. On his way home, Dingle did his best to make his rather boring, disciplined mind move to more creative, sickening application.

At this juncture of the narrative, prior to sinking into the abyss of the real horrors and weirdness of the story, it is best to fill in the remaining, some might even say boring details, concerning Dingle Dickinson's work.

He was a construction engineer and, truth to tell, quite exceptional in his field. He spent as much time on site as he did in the site office. Roughing it satisfied the essence of his natural character and his own physical need to extend, in some way, his massive frame to some degree of manual endeavour.

It would serve well to dwell on this for a moment, explain more fully, for in so doing, it might well make the man's actions to follow a little more understandable, if not exactly forgivable.

In this, the heart of it all; of little girls, stupid names, dollies and …. violence.

Draw near and prepare to weep.

I said weep … not laugh!

The two acts of physical exertion Dingle would employ, and then only when alone on site, were to throw and bend things; throw bricks and bend metal. In the course of what could have been interpreted as violent acts, he released his pent-up anger, as he called out over and over again his stupid Christian name. Also, that of his aforementioned sister, Penelope; his older and, back in the day, big sister. A fair enough name no doubt, but not one that would necessarily inflame the male passions.

Now, Penelope had a very special place of 'hate' in Dingle's memory. She not only used to tease him constantly by calling out his Christian name, but whilst doing so, giving his head a good thwack with whichever dolly she had in her hand at the time.

So, one could say there were four component parts to the machinery that really drove Dingle Dickinson to war against his very own little "Shirley Temple": his Christian name, his big sister Penelope, the dolls he was always being thwacked with in his infant years and, of course, Clara Bo Dickinson herself. Eat your heart out, Freud, give Jung the news.

You will doubtless observe that Dingle's wife didn't really feature at all. The reason for that was simple, and simply put: self-sufficient. Jayne Dickinson had become, through choice and force of circumstance, the self-sufficient housewife and mother. What magic there had been in her marriage had evaporated. She treated her husband as part of the furniture, and as a sort of family "pet" at best, and Clara Bo (Claire to her, you'll remember) as a "nice" thing to have about the house, and a welcome break from everyday matters such as cooking, cleaning, mending, the Mothers' Guild and evening classes.

And there you have it. The principal characters of the tragedy to be and the scenario. The weirdness? Yes, well that's about to commence – as of now.

Dingle arrived home from work one evening in an excellent frame of mind. With his friend's help, he had decided on the "weapon" to be used against his daughter, and the exact manner of its use.

Jayne was far too occupied with her life and thoughts to realise the difference in her husband's changed attitude to their little spouse. At the very least, it was warm and accepting. At best, it was even jovial. Clara Bo herself was quick to note, though not entirely comprehend, daddy's change of heart towards her. That was until a few days on when, at the little treasure's bedtime, it began.

Little daughter, bathed and ready for bed, was presented to father in the time-honoured ritual of 'kiss daddy goodnight' time. It was then that Dingle grabbed daughter's little dolly, ripped off the right leg and whispered dire warning into the little "treasure's" ear'ole.

'You make one untoward noise this night, or at morn's first light, and the bogeyman will come and take off yer leg! Got it!!?

The nasty, hate-saturated words went to the tiny heart as straight and true as any arrow.

A face, scrubbed and angelic, disintegrated into a small red, wobbly mass, as a brave little soul fought hard to hold back the tears. Mother hadn't heard the dire threat, only seen one of dolly's appendages come away in daddy's hand. She obviously took that 'accident' to be the cause of her little treasure's distress, and so moved in to console accordingly.

Interestingly to relate, daughter didn't tell mummy the truth as to what daddy had done and said. Perhaps the little mind was too numbed by the traumatic experience.

Still, time heals most things, one exception being abused dollies!

In the darkness of her small bedroom, Clara Bo Dickinson wept as she buried herself deep down in her bed. Her thoughts were very focussed. 'Naughty daddy. Nasty, horrible daddy!'

Late into the night, a silence over all. Jayne Dickinson noted it, as did daddy Dingle, as he allowed himself a very smug, self-satisfied grin.

Battle won? Perhaps ... but what about the war!?

II

The dark of the small room, wherein a little child did lay, not asleep, but awake and sniffling. Also, not alone, for something else was present.

Clara Bo had been so wrapped up in her own misery, that she hadn't had time to give attention or thought to anything else. However, as the night progressed, her sniffles lessened and, as a result, she became aware that there were other sniffles to be heard within the room – other than her own. Someone else – *something else* – was alone, sad and weeping.

Poor little Clara was afraid to call out for her mummy, for obvious reasons, and too scared to actually try and flee the room, and too curious to hide beneath the blankets.

At some hour within the depths of the night, it came forth. Came to Clara Bo Dickinson: the bogeyman.

Things were never to be the same again: ever.

To Clara's absolute surprise and greatest joy, he turned out to be very kind, warm, gentle, thoughtful and understanding.

Strange in shape, too dark in shadow to reveal any real features, and much saddened by how the parents down the ages had so maligned his character. But, for one little girl, he would become companion and protector. That any, parents included, who threatened her harm or discomfort, would incur his wrath.

A fresh new day. Dingle Dickinson awake before the alarm clock sounded, full of life and vigour. Perhaps the quiet of the night, the silence of that ghastly daughter, had given him a new found strength, made him feel a new man.

Dingle sprang from his marital bed, set to fight all the problems the new day might have in store for him. He immediately fell flat on his face. Well, however good the intentions, it's not at all easy facing the world on just one leg, especially when you had every right to believe that you had two; most certainly when you went to bed!

The noise of Dingle's bulk crashing down into an undignified heap on the bedroom floor awakened Jayne most rudely. She found the unexpected sight of her husband prostrate upon the floor most amusing.

'My God,' she exclaimed, 'do be a bit less noisy!'

Hubby's reply was far more personal and to the point.

'Dear God, woman, me bloody leg's missing!!'

'Don't be such a bore, darling,' replied the wife by way of sleepy response, 'you've got another one!'

Dingle Dickinson did not go to work that morning. He had problems. Jayne handled the drama with remarkable aplomb, not to mention a certain callousness.

'Don't go on so, Dick,' she chided, as hubby was definitely in whinge mode. 'Once you've had your breakies, you can go and see the Doctor. I'm sure he'll know what to do. Anyway, are you sure you came to bed with it last night!?'

Ah, the beloved logic of the female mind.

Clara Bo had looked on in amusement and interest at her daddy's empty right trouser leg. The more so as she was of mind enough to realise it had been her dolly's right leg that he had so cruelly yanked off. Mother had simply counselled her that it would be impolite to actually mention the absent appendage.

Contrary to Mrs Dickinson's expectations, the good Doctor was at a loss as to Mister Dickinson's dilemma.

'Why goodness gracious me, what a clean severance we have here, Mister Dickinson, sir!'

Other such remarks, in the same accent, followed. Definite, but not at all constructive.

Dingle was advised to go home, take an aspirin, a few days off work and not to worry unduly. After all, he had another leg!

For two days all was quiet in the Dickinson household. Father contemplated the traumatic, albeit painless loss of an essential limb, Jayne having the occasional chuckle to herself about the comic aspect to it all, and little daughter trying to understand the mystery of it all, and forsaking that puzzle, warming to the thoughts relating to her new friend and protector from the dark; Mister Bogeyman.

III

Dingle Dickinson's courage matched his physique and character, plentiful and rough. Within the week he was back at his work, sans a limb and equipped with a walking stick. For a few days he refused to compromise, spending as much time on the site as in the drawing office. Tragic, really. A few headlong dives into the mud-filled pits, death-defying balancing acts on the girders, and too many well-meaning Irishmen offering to lob off the other singular leg to 'even things up a bit!'

So it was that early one afternoon, Dingle Dickinson returned home, seething with a burning anger and resentment, covered in foul smelling mud and cursing every Irishman North of Kilburn!

Matters were not helped any when the sick-bag sickeningly sweet, would-be "Shirley Temple" Clara Bo, insisted on singing 'On The Good Ship Lollypop' for ailing daddy.

Night. Time for bed for the nauseating little girl, still blubbering because naughty, one-legged daddy had uttered bad, bad words to her favourite, one-legged dolly.

Jayne acted as mediator.

'For heaven's sake, Dick, it isn't Clara's fault you lost your silly old leg! Kiss and make up.' You will note Jayne had spoken the name Clara. A bad omen, perhaps?

With great effort and self-control, much to be admired by other fathers so sorely tested by their infant spouses, Dingle began the 'kiss and make up' routine with daughter. That was until the little beast thrust her mutilated dolly into daddy's face, insisting that he kiss and make up with *it* also, and not forgetting to apologise for the injury he had caused it.

Something in daddy's mind snapped, and he grabbed the aforementioned dolly and hurled it across the room. Little daughter, in an incredible act of forgiveness, retrieved dolly, in silence, and took it once more to daddy, cooing gently to it that daddy had accidently dropped it.

This action almost brought on an apoplectic fit upon Dingle. As Clara presented it once more to daddy, Dingle grabbed the doll and proceeded to rip off its remaining leg. Poor little Clara remained silent as she briefly looked hard at her daddy, totally stunned at the violent act, then let rip with all the power her little lungs could muster; which just happened to be quite considerable. It should also be noted that she had done so straight into Dingle's right ear.

Daddy gave a basically similar sort of cry, but far more powerful and heartfelt, as he grabbed at his right ear and went crashing backwards, then sideways out of the chair and eventually sprawling over the floor in a passable imitation of wall-to-wall carpet!

Mother did her best once more to soothe both troubled hearts, but to no avail. One broken-hearted "Shirley Temple" retreated to her bedroom, still wailing away, whilst father bemoaned the probable loss of his right ear-drum, to go with his "lost" right leg. It didn't help matters when Jayne pointed out how thoughtful daughter had been in keeping to the right side!

Father retired to bed, sans right leg and a ringing in his right ear; daughter with tear-filled, red-sore eyes, a pounding little heart and a growing feeling about her daddy: *hate*!

In the middle of the drama, the wife. She couldn't help seeing the funny side of it all.

Father lay in bed, bemoaning the loss of his right leg and, most probably, soon to be the hearing in his right ear.

At the heart of the emotional turmoil, Jayne. In spite of all, she still couldn't help seeing the funny side of it all.

In the dark of the small bedroom, little daughter found comfort, solace and friendship from the night's stranger: the bogeyman. She spoke to him about daddy's latest outrage, and how her favourite dolly had suffered further humiliation.

'Never mind, Clara,' whispered her friend from the dark, 'to each his just due.'

The little "Shirley Temple" of Cedar Cul-de-Sac didn't understand the essence of that observation.

Another morn. A rather lighter Dingle awoke, sat up, rubbed his eyes and prepared to get up. He threw back the bedclothes on his side and made to swing his singular leg out of the bed. Oops, NO LEG! NO LEGGIES!!

Dingle lost his cool, and made known, to his slowly awakening wife, his plight, in no uncertain manner.

'ME LEG!!'

The harshness of the awakening didn't put Mrs Dickinson in the most sympathetic of moods, but a certain humour did not desert her.

'Dick! You really must get out of the habit of losing things!'

Poor Dingle was struck dumb by his wife's display of a total lack of concern for his horrendous predicament. It was fully a minute before he could voice his plight more fully.

'Dear God, woman, I'm being decimated!!'

Practical as ever, Jayne assessed the situation and then gave comment.

'Yes, dear, I see what you mean. Such a waste.'

'What?,' retorted husband, not quite getting the gist of his wife's line of thinking.

'The slippers, darling,' clarified the wife. 'The ones mother bought you for Christmas. And then there are all your shoes and boots. Such a waste.'

That material assessment of his desperate situation shattered Dingle. Suddenly all strength of purpose and resolve evaporated. He slumped back on his pillows. Silly thing to do really. Without his leggies, his point of balance was somewhat adrift and, of course, he sort of …. well, sloped off the bed and bang on to the floor.

'Stop sulking, Dick, and come back to bed,' was his wife's only reaction to that mishap.

Whilst poor Dingle attempted to answer his wife's call, obnoxious little daughter entered the bedroom, having being awoken by the terrible noises that daddy had been making. She was not at all perturbed about the further plight her father had found himself in. Quite the opposite. A: she seemed to accept it, even have foreknowledge of it, and B: be amused by it.

'Oh, daddy,' exclaimed sickening daughter, in a totally unconvincing way, 'you've got no leggies.'

As daddy Dingle already knew this to be so, he didn't make direct reference to it, but merely suggested, in rather crude terms, that Clara Bo go and play with herself.

No sooner had the little dear gone to do her daddy's bidding, although not in the literal way he had suggested, mother had stern words with father, who, by this time, had just completed his ascent back on to the bed.

'That wasn't a very nice thing to say to our precious daughter, Dick!'

To reinforce her view, she gave her errant husband a none too playful rap around his ear. This resulted in the hapless man losing his tenuous hold on the bedclothes, thus plunging once more to the floor with a resounding wallop.

The day that followed was grim indeed. Dingle refused point blank to go to the Doctor a second time. He was sure it was all just a bad dream from which he would shortly awaken. Jayne constantly admonished her little darling for continually staring at her daddy; that it was impolite to do so, not to mention a sign of bad breeding.

Matters weren't helped as, from time to time throughout the day, little daughter would enquire of daddy as to where his leggies had gone. For a walkies, maybe?

There was also, of course, the more practical problem to contend with; that of moving daddy about, as he refused to stay in bed, and was now incapacitated to a fair degree. The problem was finally resolved, bearing in mind that even without his legs, Dingle was still of considerable size and weight, by moving him about on a blanket. Always the practical one, Jayne had pointed out that it was bringing up the wooden floors and lino a treat!

The day wore on. Dingle was silent, desperately trying to understand the strange ailment that had befallen him. There was something at the back of his mind, but it was too vague and distant to identify.

It was a strange sight. Dingle in his state, sitting and brooding on the blanket, whilst wife and daughter pulled and dragged him about, whilst also trying studiously – with guidance coming from Jayne – to avoid the subject of the ailment.

Evening drew nigh. Bedtime approached. Mother supervised the washing of her little treasure, before sending her, clean, fresh and ready for bed, to her somewhat decimated daddy, sitting, after a fashion, in his favourite chair. Time for goodnight kiss and cuddles.

In view of everything, perhaps not the best of ideas.

Clara had her much loved, mutilated dolly in hand. Dingle, now subconsciously wary of this pending ritual, was ready to grit his teeth and pay a certain homage to the wretched thing.

Daughter approached with a different scenario in mind. Catching her daddy completely by surprise, she proceeded to thwack him about the head with dolly. It was big, bullying sister Penelope and her infernal dolls all over again. Dingle let out a scream of rage and, in so doing, fell out of his chair and crashing, yet again, headlong to the floor. But not before he had exacted swift revenge.

It all happened so quickly. Screams and crashing. Then silence. Daddy sprawled out on the floor, daughter standing back, looking in bewilderment at her dolly, now sans both its arms! To her mother's surprise, and a certain trepidation within her father, the child went to her bed strangely silent, defiant, and with dolly in hand. She had also given her daddy a most peculiar look. Bo was extracting revenge on him for his mistreatment of her dolly, Dingle had confided as such to his wife, but Jayne had dismissed it as a fantasy, paranoia, and only said to spite their little "treasure".

Whatever the reason, Dingle Dickinson sat up in bed that night, and with the aid of several large pillows, quite determined not to fall asleep. Hour passed upon hour, the bedside clock ticked on as the good wife slept soundly on. All was warm, so warm. Eyelids began to droop, and then to close, as sleep itself beckoned. Dingle Dickinson went bye-byes.

Another morning. Suddenly Dingle was awake and aware. He went to rub the sleep from his eyes, and in so doing came to realise that another problem had entered into his fast fragmenting life: NO ARMS!!

However, on this occasion, brave daddy exercised a little more calm and thought.

Dingle decided that two heads were better than one, so gently nudged his wife with his shoulder until she began to awaken. As best he was able, Dingle informed her that his two other main appendages had departed in the night: his arms. Jayne just mumbled about not worrying, that they could look for them later.

In sad resignation, Dingle managed to roll gently on to his side and attempt to sleep just a little longer before awakening fully to the latest episode of his never-ending nightmare. In so doing, he found himself staring over to the bedroom door. There, standing still and silent, mutilated dolly in hand, was little daughter: Clara Bo Dickinson. Her eyes were very, very bright, her face very, very flushed, with a faint smile about her red ruby lips.

Surely now, daddy would love both her and her dolly.

'If you come a step nearer to me, I'll do for yer!!'

The threat from daddy was whispered, but clearly heard and understood. Daughter left, dolly in hand, and returned to her bedroom.

For an hour or so, as wife slept on, Dingle contemplated upon his situation.

Sans armies, sans leggies, much probies! Problems, that is.

IV

As it was a Sunday, it was the policy of the Dickinson household that all should indulge in an extra hour in bed, prior to leaping out to face the day. Once, seemingly an age ago, it had also been a time for a little naughties betwixt Dingle and Jayne.

This morning, as with those immediately past, was somewhat muted.

Jayne maintained her humour throughout.

'No naughties this morning, I take it?'

Hubby looked on, all silent, hurt and faintly disgusted.

'Oh well,' responded Jayne, 'let's look on the bright side.'

'What!?,' retorted Dingle.

'Money,' answered Jayne, in her best thrifty mode. 'We'll bundle all the clothes you'll no longer be needing into a sack and sell them.'

Poor old Dingle all but choked on that one.

'Good grief, woman!,' he cried aloud. 'Can't you see I've got no arms or legs!?'

'Of course I can, dear,' answered Jayne in a calm, matter-of-fact way. 'I'm not blind you, know.'

She then proceeded to explain her plan of action.

'With the money we get, we can buy some new clothes for Clara, and perhaps a new dolly. After all, you broke the one she has.'

Dingle was dumbstruck. Insult to injury and all that. He was definitely not a happy Dingle.

And so the day progressed. The wife was a little surprised that Clara was keeping to her room, but thought it was probably for the best, what with daddy and everything. Even so, she went forth to have a word with her little "treasure". In conversation, a few things were let slip, veiled half-truths uttered. Jayne began to get the queasy feeling that there just might be something to the insane suggestions her husband had uttered. Still, there was nothing she could really do about it. As long as she and her very own little "Shirley Temple" got on well, all was right with the world.

Early evening. Once more that strange smile about little daughter's lips, that certain look in her eye. It annoyed daddy, so yet again, and somewhat unwisely, he uttered threats to her person. However, his enforced caution of reserve was duly exercised. He in no way molested what was left of Clara's favourite dolly, not that he really had the means to do so.

Another night. Daddy dutifully bade his daughter goodnight, in a very chaste, apprehensive manner. She gave him a short, sharp, dry kiss on the cheek, playfully patted his ample stomach and departed to bed, but not before she'd taken a few slices of bread and jam with her, for 'her friend'.

In dead of night, Clara and her strange companion of the dark spoke, as he also munched away on his bread and jam. It was agreed that, although daddy had improved a little in attitude, it had still been wrong for him to have uttered such threats of violence towards his spouse, and that a further form of retribution had to be visited upon him. It was in the course of this conversation, that the bogeyman made it known he was lonely, wanting companionship of someone a little more senior in years. A mate, as he tastefully phrased it to his little friend, whom he guarded so dutifully. Clara didn't really understand, but said she would give it great thought, and that maybe even mummy might be able to help.

Another morning. Jayne awoke to a strange, rather faint sound, not unlike a distant sobbing. She made to turn over on to her back. As she did so, she heard a slight bumping of something landing on the floor. She sat upright very quickly and caught sight of her husband's head bouncing along the floor, coming to an enforced stop against the far wall, face towards the bed.

'Oh, Dick!,' exclaimed Jayne, 'Haven't you gone far enough!?'

Poor Dingle cried aloud in shock, despair and utter grief. However, as he was now sans lungs, all he could actually emit were faint, barely audible squeaks.

Jayne got out of bed and, with a certain degree of gentleness, picked up Dingle, or rather what remained of him, and carried him back to the marital bed. As she did so, he actually managed to conjure up a brief spark of humour.

'I'm afraid that's the naughties gone for a burton, old thing!'

It was an excellent display of valour in the face of adversity, but quite wasted, as all Jayne heard were a few pitiful squeaks.

Even so, the good wife was ever practical.

'Oh well, darling,' she twittered, just think of the money we'll save on food!'

That statement on the future economic outlook for the Dickinson household cut Dingle to the quick, so it did.

Dingle, the head thereof, that is, decided to remain in bed, or rather on the pillow, for the day. Wife went forth to do the usual household chores and look to little Clara.

In view of the latest mishap to her daddy, daughter was more than helpful and dutiful on this particular day. Strange. Mother tried to prepare the little one for daddy's much reduced state, and when dutiful daughter saw for herself, she seemed to take it all extremely well. She even offered to spoon feed him some soup to keep body and soul together, in a manner of speaking. As to where the soup would go was another matter.

It wasn't long before Clara discarded her dolly and contented herself with carrying her daddy's head about. Although not best happy with this, he couldn't actually voice his displeasure as such; leastways, nothing that would be *heard*!

Jayne thought it all rather sweet, although she was concerned that Clara might be running a temperature. That she looked rather flushed in face, her eyes seemingly just a tad too bright, wide and staring. Had Jayne looked in the mirror at herself ......

Somewhere along the way, Clara believed she at last had power over her daddy, enough to deem it safe to explain to him, or rather to what was left of him, that she, along with her strange friend of the night, had arranged the acts of retribution.

With that revelation made, Dingle Dickinson launched his last defiant act in the "war" against his nauseating little daughter. He bit the sickening little bitch's hand. Such a brave, futile final act. Vengeance was swift and lethal. Clara gave what was left of her very naughty daddy to her strange friend. A little more substantial than bread and jam, albeit just a tad too little.

Strange to tell, it wasn't until the following morning that Jayne missed what was left of her husband. But, by now she wasn't too upset. After all, he'd been disappearing in instalments for some days. Besides which, a head alone did not a husband make. Something else, truth to tell, is that with the morning's latest episode, sweet, down-to-earth, pragmatic Jayne Dickinson had taken her leave: of her senses, that is. In all she did, she was now singing to herself, as if in a world of her own, which indeed she was; in the land of the fairies. She had passed into the protective arms of madness.

In Jayne's defence, it should be put on record that she had tried to find the defecting head, but to no avail. She'd looked under the bed, in the cupboards, all about the house. She even made enquiries re the dog next door, just to make sure it hadn't got a head!

It was over. Dingle Dickinson was no more. He had decimated to the point of disappearance, with the help of Clara Bo Dickinson's friend from the night.

More nights, many nights. Jayne Dickinson was getting lonely. Little Clara could see it well enough, and thought upon her friend – the bogeyman. For his part, he also still felt lonely – and famished. Bread, jam and but a single brain did not a meal make. Daughter went forth to play matchmaker, and unbeknownst to her, provider of a takeaway – twice over!

One bright and early morning, little daughter called out to her mummy. At first, Jayne ignored the calls. Those self-same calls became the most urgent of pleas, which mother was obliged to heed. She went forth into her daughter's room.

It was not too long before the sounds of feasting could be heard.

Chomp, chomp; munch, munch. BELCH! Silence.

It had indeed been a most beneficial morning for the bogeyman. A small, rather bitter, nauseating starter, followed by a far more substantial, sweeter, seasoned main course!

End

Blow

'A what!?,' bellowed the entrepreneur in disbelief.

'A fartomusicologist, sir,' replied Nigel, his much put upon, rather sensitive assistant.

'Ye gods!,' spluttered Nigel's employer in exasperation.

Truth to tell, acts of a more exotic nature were not exactly unknown to Waldo Wotsit, for it was he who was thrown out of France for staging one of the most amazing demonstrations of a carnal nature, betwixt Lilly the little lamb and Boris, the Bull Mastiff. It put a whole spin on the act of buggery! It had been the talk of the whole country, where love, in all its forms, was all, and an art to be revered by all true Frenchmen. The first two performances had gone very well indeed. However, on the third occasion, 'Bonking Boris' got somewhat carried away in his passion and sent poor Lilly the little lamb to that far greener pasture in the sky, well and truly stuffed, with ne'er the customary Paxo in evidence! You will appreciate, I'm sure, the delicacy with which I have endeavoured to impart this sad tale to you. It was a rather messy conclusion, not to mention plain bad form, in what was, after all, a unique act.

Waldo Wosit pondered on, whilst his erstwhile assistant looked on, waiting for further instruction.

'Give me the basics again,' Wotsit demanded. 'What's his name, what *exactly* does he play, and *how*?'

'Gruntfuttock, sir. Aloysius Gruntfuttock, and he plays the Post Horn Gallop, on a post horn, sir, using his anus.'

'Christ!,' screamed out Wotsit, leaping up from his armchair.

'No, sir,' corrected the hapless Nigel, trying to be helpful, 'a post horn and his anus.'

Wotsit was now dumbstruck in disbelief, but only momentarily. He sank slowly back down into his armchair, without once taking his eyes off his timorous assistant.

'You're telling me … this Gruntfuttock fella … sticks a post horn up his arse and plays the fucking Post Horn Gallop!!??'

Ever helpful, Nigel corrected his master in the particulars of the wondrous musical ability.

'Not exactly, sir. Mister Gruntfuttock uses his anus as a means to play the instrument in question, employing his sphincter as his lips, sir. His sphincter is his embouchure, so to sp…'

Nigel trailed off his explanation, as the look on his master's face made it abundantly clear that further such details would not be welcome.

In spite of this, the hapless assistant found courage from somewhere to conclude his explanation, by noting his own appreciation of the unique musical dexterity of the aforementioned Gruntfuttock.

Silence reigned. Wotsit looked to the calendar on his oversized, penile-substitute desk. He had something on his mind: money. He then questioned further.

'Doesn't the sight of it all put the punters off their stride?,' he eventually asked of his underling.

'Not at all,' sir, responded Nigel, his enthusiasm once more restored. 'It's all done in the best possible taste. Mister Gruntfuttock performs behind a white silk screen, which is highlighted from behind by appropriate lighting, so arranged that a clear silhouette of the performer can be discreetly observed. It's quite artistic really'.

Again, the young man decided silence would be the better part of valour, so once more fell silent, whilst his master appeared to have slipped into deep thought. He was thinking on a day, a date, a location … an *event*.

Minutes passed. More still. And then Wotsit declared his intent. It would be the last night of the Proms. On that auspicious occasion, 'The Great Gruntfuttock,

Fartomusicologist Extraordinaire', would, via television and radio, astound the world with his unique talent.

The night, the event, *the* Royal Albert Hall!

Meticulous preparations had been made, the rehearsals had gone well. Aloysius Gruntfuttock was, indeed, a musical miracle of the first order. His tone and interpretation quite exquisite. Mind you, he was also a bit of the Johnny-one-note: the Post Horn Gallop to be exact. He wasn't too photogenic, either. Something of a red-faced, squat, overweight, rotund gnome. And the smell didn't help. Still, nothing a few cans of air freshener couldn't dispel. Besides which, one couldn't always have everything. There had also been two slight mishaps. Dribbles, to be a little more precise. At least the large screen hid the less savoury aspects of the musical marvel. For his part, Gruntfuttock had put it down to simply 'clearing his throat'!

And so it came to pass. The night, the event, *the* Royal Albert Hall.

Gruntfuttock was a little more red-faced and animated than usual. This was attributed to first night nerves. And then there were the more than frequent visits to the 'poopies and piddles room', as someone had chosen to describe them, that proceeded rather more "dribbles" than was usual. Still, the slightly forced positive spin was that all would be right on the night; only this *was* the night.

All was ready. The hoi polloi in the stalls, the top'n'tailed hoity toity in the gods. The event had been well publicised, and all were full of anticipation, expectation and, amidst the mass of the hoi polloi, barely disguised rebellious joy; in the assembled ranks of the hoity toity, a more than slight whiff of disgust.

The moment was at hand. It began. It was soon clear to all that it was a most excellent performance from 'Grunt', as the less than respectful referred to Aloysious. Good old Gruntfuttock was giving it his all! He was also raising a fair amount of wind from his nether region, if you'll forgive the expression. The downside of this was that such exertion was such as to make him very hot under the collar, not to mention elsewhere.

And so we come to the tragic heart of this sad, somewhat improbable tale.

Even as the unique post horn blower blew on, to such excellent effect, he was becoming more and more anxious. The climatic conclusion to the piece was but a few notes away. In true heroic 'once more unto the breach' fashion, he literally blasted his way towards that final, high note finale. Anxiety rampant, fear of a sudden failing of his back passage wind power at the last, his body afire with its own self-generated heat, came the final, sphincter-shredding 'evacuation of the bowels'

Woosh, bang, wallop and a flash of blue flame. Poor old Gruntfuttock's carcass of blubber was reduced to a mere mound of ash before the eyes of the onlookers and to a totally astounded world beyond. It was the most spectacular public display of Spontaneous Human Combustion ever recorded. Very much a case of 'bye 'bye rectum blowing fartomusicologist.

Sic transit Gloria Gruntfuttock!!

End

Bogey

(A nauseating, disgusting, vile, puke-inducing, nonsensical little tale)

Cecil Snotte was a nondescript being in character, appearance, manner and attainment. Tall, woefully thin, pasty of complexion and limited in cerebral accomplishment. A single man of thirty, still residing with, and being a burden to his much put upon parents, and eking out a living as a nondescript clerk.

Life was all but bereft of delights for Snotte, save for one thing: bogeys, oft resident within the nostrils of his somewhat large proboscis. He'd discovered the fun of 'mining' for these delights, and the consuming of, quite early in life. For the better part, he exercised caution enough to prevent his parents bearing witness to his disgusting habit, having been caught out the first few times, and receiving several severe clouts about his head as a result. At first, such retribution put an abrupt halt to the disgusting act of excavation of his proboscis; but only temporarily. Outside of his home, Cecil was far more cavalier, defiant with his habit and, as a result, received anything from verbal declarations of disgust to the occasional thwack in the mouth. Much did the lad suffer for his delights. For all this, Cecil persisted in his nauseating habit. It was not hard for him, such was his delight of the taste and texture, but perhaps we should not go there. For his part, Cecil was of the belief that anything coming from *within him*, could do no harm going back *into him*, albeit it via a different orifice!

It is quite possible that things would have continued thus, had not an unforeseen, incredible happening happened. Cecil Snotte was one day pregnant, or so it seemed outwardly. Extended stomach, morning sickness and the sudden wish for marmite, jelly and custard, within a single sandwich! In due course, Cecil was confined to his bed, being told by his parents that he 'should deal with it, and the sooner the better!' It was something of a miracle that news of Cecil's strange condition did not pass from the confines of the family home. Mind you, with this 'Tale', anything was possible.

In due course, the not-so-welcome arrival arrived. Baby bogey was born, and you shall be spared the ghastly details. Suffice to say, he, she, IT came into the world as a rather rotund, green glob of snot, with appendages, after a fashion. Arms and legs, it could be said. No facial features as such, as there was no face to speak of.

Baby bogey was confined to a dark corner in Cecil Snotte's bedroom, in a makeshift cot ... of sorts. A cardboard box, lined with a rather tatty green blanket, quite deliberately chosen, as it made the occupant all but invisible.

There was a certain tenderness to this grotesque scenario. Cecil sang to It, his baby, that is. It was still referred to as 'It', as its gender had not been determined, and no single soul was of heart or stomach enough to find out. And then there was the feeding of It. The answer as to the how of It came by way of an accident, of sorts. In a playful moment, Cecil extricated a substantial bogey from his nose and flicked it playfully at his very own issue. It landed splat on to the small green, jelly like substance, and seemed to immediately evaporate *into* it. Such was to be the way of it from thereon in.

Poor old Cecil was to be the only babysitter to the infant bogey. In reality, it simply meant sitting there and 'feeding' It as and when deemed necessary. *It* never cried out for nourishment. In truth, *It* never emitted a sound, but just laid there and gave an occasional, pathetic little wriggle. For his part, Cecil Snotte stretched his limited imagination to the limit in some sort of indulgent reverie, in which he imagined teaching his issue to play football, ride a bike, grow up and be a somebody. Things did not quite turn out that way.

One day, a relative of the family came calling unannounced, catching everybody out, as *It*, within its makeshift cot, had been allowed into the living room. The relative in question was Beryl, an emaciated streak of feminine humanity and contradictions. She had in tow her pet dog, Patch, an overfed, over-indulged, flea-infested canine, always on the lookout for food. It found some, as it slipped its leash, bounded into the living room, making its way straight for you-know-who, and consumed it whole, and all in a trice. The tragedy was not without its positives. The secret was gone before being seen by the outside world, a sort of sanity returned to the family and, from that time onwards, Cecil Snotte was freed from the disgusting habit; prospecting for you-know-what, from you-know-where.

Fast forward. Cecil Snotte going forth to think and ponder, whilst attending to his toilet. A Eureka moment followed and ….. but that's another story, for another day.

End

Stuffed!

(There are taxidermists and there are taxidermists!)

Alvin Cringe was something of a plebish non-entity. Small, squat, thin, pale and wanting in just about all things mental and physical. The poor man seemed to be an all-time loser of losers. If it rained, it seemed to fall heaviest on him; if the sun shone, it somehow managed to by-pass him; if there happened to be an accident about, looking for somewhere and someone to latch on to, Cringe was invariably the hapless victim. In character, he seemed perfect to his calling: taxidermy. He stuffed things. Just about anything and everything.

Now then, it would be very hard to find any being less attractive to the opposite sex than Cringe, but contrary to all logic, such was not the case with the misbegotten wretch. He seemed to have little trouble finding lady partners. However, let us be truthful on this point. The sort of 'ladies' he got, no self-respecting male would have, not even with the benefit of the proverbial barge pole thrown in.

Cringe found his partners of the nights by walking the streets – in dead of night. When he found one to his liking, he would whisper a little something in her ear: money. She would take his scrawny little arm and let him lead the way.

Cringe never went to his ladies' abodes, but always took them to his. That's to say, his 'second home', specifically there to entertain his ladies of the night, and to do his *own* taxidermy work. It was a small, cramped and dirty little residence. More a hovel with ideas above its station. Be that as it may, it was perfect to his needs. Here he committed his foul deeds, performed his own works of taxidermy. During the day, he was employed in the more conventional and respected field of his craft, in the company FILL-O-FAST. Stuffing deceased family pets, wildlife and such. Evenings and most weekends, it was taxidermy of an altogether darker hue.

And so, genteel readers, we come to the nasty bits of this most unlikely tale.

Alvin Cringe's second residence had all manner of shapes secreted within its shadows, still and redundant. On the walls, against the walls; hanging from ceilings and upon all manner of tables and pedestals.

All signs of the man's obsession with his calling – stuffing things: ANYTHING!

The ladies of the night who bore witness to the grim place did not go forth to announce their experiences to the world. You see, they were loved and stuffed all too quickly.

That was Cringe's true obsession. Stuffing the female of the species. Twice over, if you get my drift. I pause for just a moment to apologise for employing such an indelicate turn of phrase. However, I am sure you'll appreciate it could have been a great deal worse.

Throughout the grim establishment were no fewer than twenty ladies of the night; all well and truly stuffed. They were employed as door-stops, coat racks, draft excluders and … well, I do not think it prudent nor in good taste to go further in that direction.

Alvin Cringe's pride and place went to his late, unlamented wife. A wizened old cow who had married him in the mistaken belief that he was a person of substance, position, and … *money*. The marriage had lasted barely a year, each month beyond the first, a lifetime of hell for Cringe. At least she now served a practical, most useful purpose; a means by which he could park his bike in the hallway!

The essence of this tale is also its end. Justice, retribution, call it what you will.

Now, for the edification of you all, I relate it. Stunningly simple, horrifically gruesome.

One night, Cringe picked up, metaphorically speaking, the most hideous hag of the night it had ever been *his* good fortune to meet. He'd taken her to the allotted place and prepared to perform in the usual manner. In this particular instance, he simply wasn't *up* to it: literally! The sight of the thing, divested of all clothing, was completely off-putting. She, for her part, was none too pleased. A woman scorned and all that.

To stop her stream of curses and denouncements, Cringe proceeded to despatch her and stuff her – post haste.

He really should have paid greater attention to the hag's words – those curses. They were for *real*. You see, she was a witch.

It took the latest deceased hag of the night a little time to break the bonds that bound her. Release came one very dark, stormy night. Once free, she roamed the house, freeing the other unfortunate sister hags from their enforced imprisonments.

On this night of nights, it so happened that Alvin Cringe was at the establishment, sleeping and alone. He was destined never to awaken, in the conventional sense.

Suffice to say that the released band of night's hags went forth and did unto him as he had done unto them.

End

Imagination's Child

She had dreamt of motherhood from her earliest years. Her maternal instincts were beyond the normal. They were obsessive. As soon as she was physiologically able, she made herself available to bring about pregnancy in the most natural way. There were drawbacks to this. To begin with, her age alone. Even so, as the years progressed, it became her features, build and general demeanour that held back the better part of the male populace from declaring anything akin to feelings of love and desire, let alone fornication for its own sake, even with such bribes as money and alcohol. As one wit unkindly observed, she was a premature hag of the night, come before her time.

There were a few occasions when some males made play with her, but were unable to fulfil her need. For all this, the drive within her remained undiminished. The more so, if that were possible. She wanted a child, *from her own body*, and in the most natural of ways.

And then came the tests, upon which, the findings. The woman's screams of anguish, upon hearing the results and prognosis, could be heard throughout the hospital. Her abject despair was unnatural in its intensity. She was barren.

In the dark recesses of her tortured mind, the fire and drive of her imagination became even greater. Phantom pregnancies were frequent. She gathered all manner of things for a baby that would never be. Her conversations with the imagined infant were never ending. Such friends as she had, feared for her sanity, and theirs. The years passed, time ravaged her body, her features the more so. She became all but destitute.

At some point along the downward spiral that was her journey through life, she took up companionship with a male vagrant. They were often seen about the streets. A strange, tragic sight to behold. He carrying their pitifully few possessions, she pushing an old, battered and previously discarded pram she had acquired, croaking lullabies to an infant that only she could see.

Yet, cannot imagination be father to whoever or *whatever* it wishes?

Forces moved and night prepared to be midwife to the spawn of a fevered mind.

The rain fell, driven by the wind, accompanied by a rumbling in the heavens and within the bowels of the earth below.

A rain-drenched, derelict building, greatly exposed to the elements, was to be the delivery ward. The woman, now prostrate upon the floor, soiled rags as linen, soon to be swaddling cloth for an infant from the dark. Sat on his haunches, some distance away, her hapless, increasingly fearful vagrant companion watched on, in no way party to the creation about to make its entrance.

The pain was becoming greater, more blood flowed, but the woman was lost in the ecstasy of impending birth. For her, the pain was almost orgasmic in its intensity.

Then, in the final phase, amidst the madness of it all, a moment of absolute, coldly insane clarity, a truth made clear … and then … the *birth*.

It ripped and tore itself through the birth canal and out into an unsuspecting world. It left its mother a bloody, ripped and torn carcass, no more a living being. Her dying screams reverberated through the labyrinths of Hell. Then silence, save nature's own storm of protest and the whimpers of an unseen infant.

The woman's vagrant companion had fled into the safe, dark anonymity of the night. In a short time, something akin to guilt took a hold on him, and he sought out the nearest Police station, informing the duty officer that a lady had much need of help.

Before too long, Medicine and the Law were in attendance in the depths and teeth of a foul night. They gazed on at the bloody mess splayed out on the filthy rags. Whoever she was, whatever her sins in life may or may not have been, she had not deserved such an end. No human did.

With as much gentleness and tenderness as they could muster, the ambulance men removed the mortal remains and transported same to the hospital. The Police Inspector had ordered it so, requesting a post mortem as soon as it was possible. In the meantime, he had questions to put to the deceased's male companion, answers to find.

As the light of a new dawn spread out over the sky, and the darkness surrendered to the approaching day, some vague, half-light of knowledge came slowly to those in the small room within the Police station. But it was so vague, lacking in any real substance. A little too much by way of supposition, short on fact. Was the vagrant mad? Had his lifestyle over the years addled away his senses?

Of one thing all were sure, he lacked the capacity for imagination.

The man did not seem to be of wit or reason enough to concoct such a story. Yet, his terror was real enough, as were the details as to the description of the woman, her state and where she was to be found.

Over the days that followed, the foul weather persisted, as those charged with such business continued to try and piece together the history of the tragedy. The late woman's companion had died only hours after speaking what he knew of the woman to the Police. His final, half insane mutterings were not, *could not* be taken seriously.

The post mortem had itself given birth to far more questions than it had answers. The woman *had* given birth, but to what the experts could not determine. The trauma of the delivery had brought about her death. The most unbelievable statement of fact presented to the investigating officers was also the most unacceptable. How could they accept it? If the experts were to be believed, the woman had died a virgin.

Later into another foul night. The senior investigating officer was wrestling with three key questions. What was the truth of it all, how could he bring closure to the case and what, if anything, did the woman actually bring into the world? The officer decided he needed to once more view the scene of the tragedy.

The driver waited in the car whilst one of Scotland Yard's finest tried to make sense of it all. Yet madness has no sense to speak of. The sounds of the wind and the lashing down of the rain made it almost impossible for the officer to listen out for any *other* sounds. Something. He did hear something. He was sure that he had. Somewhere in that ruin that was once a house of some size, *something* lurked.

Again, the sound. A weeping? An occasional word?

A desperate feeling entered into the officer. There were things best not heard, revealed. This was no longer the place for any Christian soul to dwell. There *was* a presence. It withered the soul, made redundant Christian beliefs.

The officer felt weak and nauseous. Even as he turned to leave, the cry rang out clearly above the sounds of the elements. The cry of a lost, unblemished, newborn soul.

When the officer did not return to the car, the driver braved nature's forces and went forth to find him, and did so. The man was on the ground, having being overwhelmed by something beyond comprehension.

As the driver struggled to assist his senior colleague to his feet and away from the wretched place, once more the cry of desperation rang out. The driver thought he heard, but did not heed. Best not always to turn and see what behind doth tread.

Alone once more, Imagination's Child. The gross enfant terrible, it its final moments of utter, abject despair, spoke muted supplication.

'Into Thy care, O Lord, my abandoned soul.'

The pitiful utterance was drowned in the sounds of the lashing rain and the howling wind.

End

'Charlie Mumbles'
(or: 'SQUAWK!')

Parrot Extraordinaire

Fred and Freda Mumbles had been married for the proverbial 'Forty years, and not a day too long'. They had been made for each other. The kids long gone their own way, but friends aplenty. Fred was no longer the man he was, physically, and retirement loomed large. Freda, only a few years younger, but both had sufficient vim and vigour to their needs in the Autumn of their lives. They had enjoyed a few pets along the way, but Flossie, the Basset hound, had been their favourite. They had her for more than sixteen years. Then, one day not so long past, Freda had found their beloved mutt in the kitchen, alongside her food bowl. On her back, stiff as a board, leggies straight up in the air; dead as a dog's dinner.

The departure hit Fred and Freda hard, the former the more so. Fred, still a security guard, had been a strong and able man in his youth, and for most of his adult life, and took the slings and arrows of life pretty much in his stride. Even so, he had admitted to his close mates that he'd dropped some snot and snivels on that day.

Time passed. Both Fred and Freda did think about another pet, but not a dog, as no other mutt could replace their irreplaceable Flossie. Odd to say, thought Freda at the time, Fred had made brief passing mention of a parrot. Freda on the other hand, did display a certain glint in her eye at the passing suggestion. Then, one day, one of Freda's friends, Joy, tricked Freda into going into a pet shop, and there beheld, for the first time, up close and personal, a parrot. Lord knew why, but she took an instant liking to it. She was informed by Joy that it had been taken in by the shop only days after its previous owner had keeled over; kaput.

Then Joy, with the aid of the shop keeper, informed Freda that the former owner had only had the parrot a week or so. But, even in that short time, had grown very fond of it. As she'd told her friends, it had a certain way about it where humans were concerned. The previous owner had called it 'Three-Ps' for Pretty Polly Parrot. Freda was up for it, but that stupid name had to go. By its way and look, she thought it a bit of a Charlie.

That was it! She decided to try and persuade Fred to buy it, beginning the process by naming it Charlie Mumbles. She was sure that would help the cause.

To her surprise, the shop owner offered to throw in the cage that had come along with it for good measure, explaining that neither had cost him a penny. As Freda had pointed out, the said cage was almost as big as her living room. Not quite so, as Joy *knew* it would fit snuggly into the front window alcove of the Mumbles living room, which itself was of a more than adequate size.

For its part, unbeknownst to Freda, Charlie Mumbles *would* be bound for the Mumbles home, together with cage, a supply of food and a few toys to play with. Such would be gifted to a much surprised and delighted Freda, if, in her belief and planning, she could persuade Fred to purchase the fowl of the air.

It was then Joy had suggested she and Freda repair to a nice little café not too far away, have something to eat and plan a strategy as how best to persuade Fred of the benefits of purchasing a very particular 'lodger'. Whilst on their way, Joy had made a simple, very brief call, on her mobile. The subterfuge was progressing nicely.

Time moved leisurely on. Meal consumed, and the strategy in place, Joy said she'd walk back with Freda, in case she felt need for moral support.

And then it happened, the truth revealed. As they approached the Mumbles residence, Joy called out. In moments, Fred had stepped out of the house to greet the ladies, enquiring to Joy as to how 'it' had all gone, which she did, by way of a positive, beaming smile. Fred gave a strange reply; something about it all 'being in place'.

With Freda on the verge of protesting, Fred, somewhat unusually, put his arm around his other half and began guiding her firmly, but lovingly, into the house, Joy following behind, giggling in joy and anticipation.

Freda had hardly walked through her front door when she heard it. A squawk, and knew in an instant. Before she could question, Fred had got her to the open living room door and pushed her in, as she instinctively looked immediately towards the front window, with her eyes settling instantly on cage and content, emitting a delighted sort of human squawk of her own, not to mention tears from her eyes.

Her emotions were reciprocated parrot wise, literally, as Charlie Mumbles extraordinaire, made known her own delight. A cacophony of joyous sounds resounded around the room and beyond, with both Fred and Joy joining in.

So, in simple telling, what was Charlie Mumbles actually like in look and manner? Herewith, the relevant details.

Well, for a start, if it looks, sounds and acts like a parrot, it is, indeed, a parrot. But, oh, so, so much more.

Charlie Mumbles was a blue and gold macaw, possessed also of a squawk that would put a foghorn to shame, and was yellow of eye. And its own personal place of residence was a very large cage, prominently placed in the alcove in front of the large bay window. The door of the said cage was, on all but rare occasions, always to be left open. Freedom ruled – OK! As to moving about the house; anywhere and everywhere, including her own chauffeurs. That's to say, the shoulders of both Fred and Freda. It was a sign of both love and good manners, that Charlie never pooped on either! As to moving about under her own wing power, it was an art and sight to behold. Like a Spitfire on steroids. She could be quiet and graceful, or loud and crazy, depending on her mood. The rule is usually for parrots on the loose to take to the high places …. out of human reach much of the time. Not so

Charlie. In the Mumbles abode, she was Numero Uno. For a start, sometimes Charlie would simply walk, even stroll around, imperiously surveying her domain. As to sleep, any place, any time. Dogs? Not a chance. There was no place for any other non-humans. After all, it took Charlie a lot of time, patience and NOISE to get Fred and Freda to do and serve as she required. There was only one power in Charlie's domain, and SHE was it! Pardon? Of course she did. She loved her servile *servants* to bits. She adored them, as they did her. And for Charlie, it wasn't just cupboard love.

As to guard dogs, forget 'em. Nothing Charlie couldn't do, and better. Remember the analogy to the Spitfire? For good reason. Dive bombing and squawking. And, if she thought her own (that's Fred and Freda) were in any danger, the beak and claws came into action. Meeting Charlie in her own domain for the first time was an experience in itself. If one survived that, it meant you were accepted by the Mistress of the Domain: Charlie! Joy was most definitely one of the few so accepted into the fold.

If things don't change, they remain the same. Such was the case in the Mumbles home. One day, whilst reading his newspaper, Fred suddenly felt tired, feeling need of a catnap. He did, only it was a little longer than he'd expected. He died.

The process of mourning, burial and continuance of life unfolded; for Freda, that is. She had Joy and a few others to help and support her. Also, of course, Charlie Mumbles.

Over the days, weeks and months that followed, Charlie Mumbles was there to cheer and comfort Freda. Not so much by her side, more either in her lap or on her shoulder. The occasional time, to give her now beloved, sole owner, a little joy, she'd perch on Freda's head; ever so gently, no hint of claw or beak. The latter, only if she were gently muzzling the lady's cheek, and which Freda much appreciated.

Fred's departure was not that much of a shock. Freda could sense it coming. Energy slowly draining away, slowly departing his aged limbs. Perhaps the best indicator of the coming closure of his life being that Charlie Mumbles spent a lot more time in Fred's lap or on his shoulder. She'd desisted perching on the dear old man's head. Even at bedtime, Charlie took to laying close on Fred's side of the bed.

For the better part, it was now more or less just Freda and Charlie, although Joy popped in at least a few times a week, and kept in touch by 'phone.

And so life settled down once more, slow and gentle. That was the way of it. No fuss, no bother, no further tears after the burial. And no, Charlie Mumbles stayed at home for that one.

The local Police station was only a road away, and they knew the Mumbles household well. The Desk Sergeant, Sid, often popped in for a tea and chat. The more so when Charlie Mumbles took up residence. The Sergeant was a bird fancier; pigeons that is. Charlie Mumbles took to the Sergeant immediately, although he thought the good man whiffed a bit; of pigeons! The Sergeant had arranged for a Constable to patrol past the Mumbles house at least four times a day; twice AM, and twice PM.

Then, of course, there was Charlie Mumbles to guard house, home and Freda. Before the year was out, this proved to be so. The story to tell.

The first tentacles of winter were beginning to enwrap most things, as the nights stole in with its dark shroud. Much to the delight of .... burglars.

From the moment Fred had vacated hearth and home for a higher place, Charlie Mumbles had made it her duty always to retire to bed when her beloved Freda departed for a well-earned night of sleep. For a week or so, she did not find it too easy, Fred no longer being at her side. Charlie Mumbles rectified the matter. A simple caress of Freda's cheek from the wing of a somewhat remarkable bird, and Freda passed into a long, deep, beautiful sleep, each and every time.

And so it was to be from that first night on, with Charlie tucked in tight as she snuggled up close into Freda's back, from the outside of the top blanket.

Time marched on, as did life. Steady, regular, sans any dramas of note. And then ....

Night, cloak of darkness, most sleeping, others about their business, such as burglary. Two being rather inept beings who gave the very title Neanderthal a bad name. In the 'trade' (crime, that is), they were referred to Mess'n'Mash.

As Freda and Charlie Mumbles slept, the less than stealthy burglars approached the Mumbles abode, and then Mash performed his usual manner of entry; picking the front door lock. It wasn't the most up-to-date, and any halfway competent could have picked it without any great effort, and let us simply say Mash couldn't even spell the word; competent, that is.

Up in the bedroom, Charlie Mumbles had heard what was going on, which wasn't hard. She was up and ready, making sure that her beloved owner would sleep soundly on.

And what exactly followed is, in truth, hard to record. In the fullness of time, it was only Mess who gave some sort of account, which made no sense at all. For his part, Mash had ceased to talk to anyone after the incident. Perhaps silence wasn't that hard for him, as he'd never been able to string a coherent sentence together. Even so, in his defence, it has to be said a fundamental fear had struck him dumb: literally. If but an iota of what his partner in crime had said as regards to their experience on entering the house, it was small wonder.

According to Mess, once in the darkened house, they closed the door silently (if one could believe that of them). They then turned as one to face the stairs that led up to the bedroom. It was then it happened.

In a thrice, all the lights went on, the house ablaze in blinding light. And then there was the shrieking of what sounded like a banshee from hell. And then, upon the stairs, a young, big, fit and powerful man: Fred Mumbles in his prime.

Mess and Mash, stood together, struck dumb and terrified at what came at them. They were like a tableaux of fear. In a moment, the apparition was upon them. In but a moment, he, it, Fred from beyond, had cracked their heads together.

It was then, as told by Mess, what *appeared* to happen that stunned the listeners.

As the two hapless burglars began their one-way journey from the stairs to the floor, towering over them was ….. a 'bleedin' giant parrot', and fearsome in its countenance. As both Mess and Mash passed into the blissful state of unconsciousness, and within minutes, all but the dim hallway light, went out; just like that.

In the bedroom, Freda and Charlie Mumbles continued to sleep soundly on; the latter with a most satisfied and contented smile on her face …. Beak, that is!

In the Police station just down the road, the 'phone rang. Something about a burglary at the Mumbles home, and to get down there, fast!

This latter part of the *unbelievable* tale, even harder to comprehend, let alone believe, was verified by the Desk Sergeant of the night; Sid. He knew the voice of the late Fred Mumbles well enough, and was certain it had been he who had made the call. Well, it had to be, wasn't it? Yet, all knew Fred was long dead, wasn't he?

And that wasn't all. Before hanging up, the 'voice of Fred', had advised the Sergeant to go quietly, enter quietly, remove the "garbage" – quietly – and allow his good lady, Freda, to sleep on; also Charlie Mumbles, as she'd had a rather stressful night!

And so it was.

Needless to say, it wasn't long before word of the night's happenings got out. The story soon became the stuff of legend. As for Freda, she eventually heard ever more fanciful tellings of the event. Each and every time, she simply smiled sweetly as she went about her business.

And what of Charlie Mumbles?

Well, she simply seemed to puff out her chest a little more, and spent a little more time walking her domain, with what people observed to be a little more of a strut and swagger, often making the oddest squawks, that even Freda hadn't heard in the past. Only other parrots would be able to understand and appreciate the sentiments expressed. Something along the lines of 'Anything a male, of any species, human or otherwise, can do, we female parrots can do better, and without half the fuss!!'

*Squawk**

(*End)

Whyte

Bert Whyte arrived home late. He was in quite a state. His partner, Agatha, could smell the alcohol on his breath. Not for the first time. He wasn't the best of drivers and, after a drink or two, he was even worse. Even so, this seemed to be different. He actually seemed to be stressed. No, wonder, he'd just killed a man. Not intentionally, you understand. Simply the outcome of alcohol and his usual bad driving. It should be made known that he did not inform his partner of the tragedy. For her part, Agatha relegated him to the spare room. A little to her surprise, he departed meekly.

If Bert had departed under the proverbial cloud, come morning and he was about to enter a fucking thunder storm!

Came the morn, came the surprises, the shocks: and then some.

Alcohol can be the bringer of sleep, provide the lull before the storm. Bert slept well. However, in the awakening, reminder of the night before. Of a death. Still, he reasoned with his insane logic, it had been dark, no one had been around, bourn witness. Body probably wouldn't be discovered until the morning, it having being hurled upward, away and into the long grass of the verge. No prob. Mind you, he was reminded that his better half had been somewhat miffed at his homecoming state. He'd have to placate her. Such is but one aspect of human relationships.

So engrossed was Bert in his thoughts, that he hadn't really taken note of a somewhat peculiar oddity about his person. However, revelation was not long delayed. He looked downward for a moment, and so his new plight was revealed. His hands were black, as were his forearms. Odd. They'd been white when he'd staggered to his bed on the night past. Trick of the light, perhaps? Bert, not the brightest tool in the box at the best of times, was confused, not to say a tad scared. After all, although he would not freely admit it, he was a racist in nature. Not direct, up front with it. Too much the coward. More by innuendo, sly jibe, clumsy, so-called humour.

In reality, Bert was an obnoxious little shit, something of a waste of space. For Christ's sake, his parents had even named him after their favourite make of car; the BMW: Bertrand Michael Whyte! That's why Bert had one, old and battered though it was. His thinking was like the man – simple. If you're named after one, you might as well drive one!

For all that, he now had a more immediate problem. He rose from his bed and made his way to the dressing table mirror. Reflection would prove the normal reality of things. Not so. Bert looked on, gaping in disbelief. He, of all people, was now a black man!

Bert fled the room, seeking confirmation of his new , unwanted status, along with comfort and solace from his long suffering partner. Not a good move.

Agatha was still in a none-forgiving frame of mind. However, the moment she saw the state of her biggest mistake regarding matters concerning men, she was aghast. The more so when she was able to make out what her woe begotten mishap of manhood was bemoaning: that he was black! When Agatha decried the stupidity of the claim, as he was obviously as white, and liver-livered as when he'd poured himself into bed the previous night, Bert proceeded to remove his shorts, thus revealing his squat, rotund, bollock-naked form, in all its sickening, anaemic-white inglorious state.

The more Agatha tried to calm the idiot, the more he ranted, raged, bemoaning his situation, as he believed it to be, as he pointed to the fact. He seemed to become more and more beside himself, even demented in his manner. Indeed, Agatha was becoming fearful for her own wellbeing.

The much put upon partner need not have worried, as help was to hand, announcing itself by a strong rapping upon the door, and a call from the Law.

'Mister Whyte, Bertram Michael Whyte? We need to speak with you, sir – NOW! Open the door!'

A blubbering blob of confused, guilt-wracked, questionable manhood, and a closet racist to boot, struggled to put his shorts back on, as Agatha waited impatiently to open the door, and to a possible means of protection from a raving loon, as she was now beginning to view her partner.

And then they were there, two plain clothes officers of the Law. The one was of average height, well set and, just for the record, white. His fellow officer was something else altogether. A tall, well set, very muscular man. Those who knew about such things, saw him as the spitting image of John Barnes. Like his famous, ex-Liverpool FC favourite lookalike, this particular officer of the Law was Jamaican by birth, but even more powerfully built and imposing.. He protected both his colleagues and members of the public with due diligence, and was also fearless. He could not abide racism in any form. In such a matter, he was fearsome in his condemnation, protecting all races and religions with equal vigour, and even a sense of righteousness.

So, this particular individual, who was simply called JB by friends and close colleagues, viewed, with greatest suspicion and annoyance, the weird little man before him, who was jumping up and down in greatest distress, as he declared that he was black, having been white all the days of his miserable little life; before this morn, that is.

The first officer was carrying a laptop, which he proceeded to put on a nearby table, lifted the lid, switched on and logged on, whilst his colleague, JB as you'll recall, with a most commendable degree of calm and tolerance, advised the weird little Jack-in-the-box to still himself and be seated, and give close attendance to the laptop screen. To reinforce the instruction, JB had removed his set of handcuffs, making it quite clear that he would use them if necessary. Whilst all this was going on, Agatha had all but hidden herself behind the human brick wall that was JB, remaining silent and, within moments, transfixed by the images on the laptop screen.

To state it plainly, there, in very clear and coloured imagery, proof positive of Bert Michael Whyte's murderous drive. Of him knocking an unfortunate individual off his motorbike, sending him hurtling upward and then downward into the grass of the roadside verge. It then showed the driver of the old, somewhat battered BMW, getting out and going across to view his hapless victim. Although the latter could not be seen, the former was clear to behold. None other than Bertrand Michael Whyte, and as white in skin colour as the officers now viewed him in the flesh. Much to their disgust and displeasure. The horror was not yet concluded. As all observed, the film showed that Bert was speaking and, when over the fallen, but unseen victim, bent down to take a closer look. He then stood back upright and, as he turned to go, spoke a few more words. Although not heard on film, his lips were clear to see. He then got back in his car and sped away.

Agatha stood in abject silence, tears rolling down her cheeks, as her apology for a man sat head down and silent. Officer JB then began the coup de grace, as his colleague logged off and turned off the laptop, then closed the lid.

JB, in a cold and direct manner, informed the gob-struck moron that was Whyte, that the road they'd viewed was called, by the locals, 'the track', because of the wide but sharp bend and the long stretch of straight road that followed. In view of the accidents and fatalities the 'track' had claimed, a series of special CCTV cameras had been set up, and when linked up to one another gave front, back and side coverage … and in glorious colour.

Whyte had noted that, in the film, he was indeed a white man, but as he looked at his body, saw only black. It got worse.

JB went on to inform the hapless sap that they had a brilliant lip-reader at the station, and he had translated the two words Whyte had spoken to the victim, who by then was, in fact, dead. 'One less'.

It was over. JB requested Agatha to get the murderer some trousers, socks, shoes and a jumper. This was duly done, with JB's colleague tersely instructing the now arrested Whyte to 'make haste'. Duly dressed and handcuffed, Whyte was none too gently escorted from his marital home, which he was most unlikely to see again, ever.

As the door closed behind the departed, Agatha suddenly seemed to have a moment of epiphany. Bert was gone, she was free; free at last! She could also revert to her God-given, maiden name: **Agatha BLACKE!**

End

Fire!
The Transubstantiation of Miss Hannah

Earth

Hannah Carr had barely entered the Arrival lounge at Port-au-Prince Airport, when she was informed that there was a message for her.

Joe would not be joining her for a few days of their planned 'dream' holiday. He'd been delayed on an assignment in London. Being a photo-journalist for AP, such was nothing new.

Hannah was not best amused. Although quite capable of fending for herself, she missed her Joe, especially as this was her first visit to the country – Haiti; this earth, this land, on which the world of its inhabitants did stand. An exotic mix of sun and sea; of violence and of ... Voodoo. Even so, when Joe had told her what he had in mind, she was both surprised and delighted, and jumped at the chance of such a journey. The surprise came inasmuch as such had never entered her mind, and Joseph, his full, God-given name, had never spoken of the country in any conversation regarding holidays and travel. So, why was it, when she knew that she was to be Haiti bound, that for the first time a most peculiar sense passed through her; deep, primordial, and significant?

Now, alone on this Island of wonderment and witchcraft, to add to Hannah's concerns was the fact that for her very first night, Joe had arranged for them to go to a fire dance, but not just any old fire dance, in any old place. This was to be in the Bois Cainman, in the Northern mountains; Voodoo heartland, so said. Joe had been rather proud of this little surprise, especially as the lady of his life had been taken by her first fire dance in Thailand. The odd, once only, momentary fainting spell notwithstanding, when she returned back home, she had sought out any such enterprise, but with no success. Anyway, as she consoled herself, it would not have been the *real* thing, not in England; God bless her. For reasons she could not fathom, after Thailand, it had to be the real thing. Little did she know, when the time came once more, it would not be the fire dancing that would stun all present, wondrous and fantastic though it proved to be.

It was just after midday at the hotel. Hannah, bathed and refreshed, put on a pale cream, cotton trouser suit and rested on top of the bed. Her feelings were mixed. Glad to have arrived and settled in such an extraordinary land, but warped in the energy-sapping humidity and the resignation that Joe was not at her side.

Be that so, Joe had told Hannah that he'd taken certain steps, and that someone would be calling upon her arrival at the pre-booked hotel. Something more; she felt as though she *knew* of something to be, but not what.

It didn't take long for Hannah to start drifting in and out of the lightest of sleeps, as she allowed her thoughts to wander freely on, and from which memories of the last holiday began to surface. Of Thailand, Joe and, yes, that fire dancing! Yet for all those memories, she could not help but sense some were absent and could not be reached: yet.

It had been Joe's idea to 'go somewhere exotic', and Hannah had suggested Thailand. She'd always wanted to visit that particular country. So, the summer past, they had flown into Bangkok airport, then travelled by boat and road, enjoying the various sights of the land.

It got to Hannah. The sheer scale and beauty of it all. However, it also jarred badly against the sights, sounds and stench of poverty and deprivation. When standing in the reality of it all, and not viewing from a distance via a glossy poster, she was uncomfortable because of the humidity, smoke and dirt aspects of the surrounds. It sat ill with her. For all that, the white sands and the clear blue waters had been what all the posters had suggested and more. Also the polyglot of tourists; nationalities and positions in life, and the fact that they all seemed to mix well together within that magical, alien land environment. Such contradictions!

It was on that particular trip that Hannah had learnt first to fire dance, and for reasons she could not explain, even to herself, it seemed so *natural* for her. Although, in reality, not exactly what the term itself implied in what it was, she soon proved herself to be quite proficient. Even so, compared to what she would witness in the Bois Cainman of Haiti, her efforts were as nothing. Also, whilst the atmosphere at Ko Sammuni was one of fun and light, Bois Cainman would show itself to be of a considerably darker hue, both by the lateness of the hour and the collective mindset of the native Islanders present.

Hannah continued in twilight reverie, remembering the beautiful sights of the moon, its shimmering reflection upon the white sand and the deep blue waters. Not forgetting as well the amazing sight of the plankton, seemingly lighting up the depths of the sea.

Amidst this panoramic picture, Hannah became aware of a beating. Drums? Bongos? Hers? Her Djjembe!? No, it was the singular sound of reality breaking into her mental fantasies of something well passed. What Hannah heard was a knocking at the door. She made the effort to drag herself back to full consciousness, sit herself up and then rise from the bed. Once more, the knocking. Harder, more rapid, insistent. Signs of impatience.

'Coming,' responded Hannah, desperately marshalling her thoughts as she reached the door. 'Coming!!'

Hannah opened the door and viewed her caller. A tall, suave Englishman of military bearing. He had thinning grey hair and a deep facial tan that highlighted his grey eyes. He was soon displaying a courtesy fast fading from the world, coupled with a natural, high intelligence and a quiet, gentle humour. He was quick to realise he had disturbed the lady's slumber.

'Oh, profuse apologies, my dear. Better I come back.'

Hannah, for her part, was waking, fast!

'Not at all, sir. You only caught me cat-napping.'

Both laughed politely, as Hannah, having invited the caller in, closed the door, then turned to face the man before her.

'John Saville, Miss Hannah. A mutual friend asked that I stand in for him.

An actor past, thought Hannah, something of a film buff. The fine-looking English gentleman reminding her of such; George Sanders. Yes, that was it. In look, manner, tone and pattern of speech; just like that fine actor of yesteryear. She smiled.

Sir John Saville, Special Ambassador to the British Consulate in Haiti, reciprocated the young lady's smile.

'You have the advantage over me, Miss Hannah.'

Hannah guided her guest into the main area of the bedroom suite and to a comfortable chair as she replied.

'No, sir, you have the advantage over me, as I don't know who you are.'

Hannah invited the man to sit himself down, whilst sitting herself in another like chair opposite. In old world courtesy, the man waited for his host to be seated before he himself sat down, laughing politely, softly, with Hannah joining in.

'So I do, my dear,' confessed John Saville. My apologies. Our mutual friend, who asked that I escort you to the Bois Cainman tonight, as he cannot be here with you, is the common denominator.'

'You mean *my* Joseph?,' asked Hannah in some surprise.

'Indeed so', confirmed Saville. 'He interviewed me in London last year. I think I gave him the idea of bringing you here for a holiday. He's a nice young man. You're both, if I might proffer the opinion, well suited to one another. Joseph is not the usual hack one comes across in this day and age.'

There was no malice in the English gentleman's statement, but just the slightest mocking smile about his lips.

Hannah smiled back sweetly. Then, suddenly aware that she had lost her sense of time, looked to her watch.

'It's after four, sir. Are we late?'

Saville casually glanced at his watch, then put his charge at ease.

'No, my dear, not at all. It is I that am ahead of my schedule. I had to get a number of things done, and also meet with someone, so I have done so in such a way as to take the two most important matters together, and in the one place. I really hope you do not mind, as I've arranged to meet someone here.'

Hannah seemed to think for a moment, then smiled as she stood up, moved over to and sat on the edge of her bed, speaking as she did so, Saville looking keenly on.

'No, sir, of course not,' came the reply.

'That's very accommodating of you, my dear. You'll like her. A most remarkable woman. And we have time aplenty, by the way. The show is not until a late hour. One other thing, if I may, Miss Hannah. Just call me John, please. The handle's just for ceremony, getting taxis and decent tables in restaurants.'

Hannah looked wide-eyed when *Sir* John had made his request, and after such, a sharp in-take of breath. 'My God,' she thought to herself, 'he really is a Knight of the Realm!'

Regaining her composure, Hannah got in her own little riposte.

'Thank you, Sir … I mean …John, but I still don't know who you are.'

'You're quite right, of course, my dear, and it's very amiss of me,' responded the Knight. 'Well, formally, I am Sir John Saville, Special Ambassador to the British Consulate in Haiti. That's why your young man had interviewed me in the first place. For myself alone, I'm a rather boring old duffer, truth to tell.'

Hannah found Sir John's light, self-deprecating manner rather sweet and disarming, even comforting. Even so, she was fast piecing things together. There was a certain symmetry evident. Although she had expressed the wish for some excitement, some 'edge' to her next holiday, it had been her Joseph who had come up with Haiti, and he had never mentioned the place previously. And to top it all, enlisted a genuine Knight to safeguard his damsel whilst he was absent. 'Men! Bloody men!!,' she'd thought to herself.

'Why Haiti?,' asked Sir John, as if linking into Hannah's thoughts.

The appropriateness rather caught Hannah out, and she had to think for a moment.

'It was Joseph,' she eventually answered. 'I just wanted something a little more exciting. It was he who chose Haiti, not I, although I'm delighted he did. I hope I haven't offended at all,' she added, with some concern.

Sir John smiled. It was a reason he had heard spoken countless times.

Without really being conscious of his act, the Knight had taken a cigarette case from an inside pocket of his jacket, a lighter from one of the outside pockets and was about to proceed, when suddenly he seemed to remember something and stopped in mid-action.

'I do apologise, Miss Hannah, good manners are often the victim of bad habits.'

Hannah smiled.

'Please, Sir …. John', she responded, trying to put the man at ease, 'don't mind me. And please, just call me Hannah.'

'Thank you, Hannah, and I shall,' answered Sir John, as he put both his cigarette case and lighter back from whence they came.

'So', prompted Hannah, 'where do facts end and legend begin about this lovely Island?'

'Where indeed,' replied the Knight, almost to himself, as if his charge were not even present.

Sir John seemed to fix his attention to some point beyond the confines of the suite as he sat back and spoke, as much to himself, by way of recollections, as to Hannah.

'Well, to begin with,' he began, 'Haiti is occupied by two separate nations; the Republic of Haiti and the Dominican Republic. There was an identity crisis from the outset. Columbus landed in the Northern part in fourteen-ninety-two, thinking he'd landed in India, South East Asia. Hence, he referred to the natives he came across as *Indians*, for God's sake! In reality, they much prefer the term Tainos, meaning "men of good". In the main, very apt, for that is exactly what the Islanders are.'

Hannah had listened attentively, but could not help but interrupt.

'And "Papa Doc"?,' she innocently asked.

Sir John gave a snort of disapproval.

'A pumped up little pimp, gangster, only in power through playing on the ancient beliefs of the people, and good old fashioned muscle; his dreaded "Tonton Macoute".'

'And his son?,' queried Hannah.

'Likewise,' answered the good Knight, 'only less so, if you see what I mean. A dwarf and imbecile to boot!'

'And the magic?,' asked Hannah, hoping for something more.

'Rubbish,' responded Sir John, dismissing all that was popularly claimed for it. 'Poor Haiti,' went on the Ambassador, mellowing somewhat. 'First the Spanish, then the French. Even the Americans have had their feed, not to mention ourselves.'

'So the magic isn't true?', pressed Hannah.

'Not the rubbish peddled by the Du Valieres. The old man spoke a lot about it, yet knew little about it.'

'So there isn't magic,' teased Hannah gently, with just the hint of a smile on her face.

'Oh yes, dear lady,' retorted the Ambassador in all seriousness. 'Believe it so. Both of the Light and the Dark.'

Hannah became concerned, yet again, that she may have offended her guest.

'Oh, Sir John, I've offended you. Forgive me.'

The Knight suddenly sat forward and very upright, giving his host a reassuring smile.

'Of course not, my child. And how can you speak any other way if you have not been informed in any other way?'

Hannah was relieved.

There was moment or two of silence, then Hannah spoke again.

'Thank heaven,' she said, 'but I must say, I find it hard to believe. We live in an age of science and reason ... and enlightenment.'

'Yes, quite so,' seconded Sir John, as one might appease and comfort a child.

'And what about tonight, John, and the Bois Cainman?,' queried Hannah.

Sir John once more sat back and settled in his chair, smiling knowingly at his young host as he began to answer.

'What indeed. You may recall that it's in the Northern mountains; home of Voodoo. The *real* thing, I hasten to add.'

In truth, Hannah didn't know what to believe, save that she was excited.

'And this lady friend of yours, John, will she come? Is she a Voodoo lady', asked Hannah by way of an afterthought.

Sir John gave a tolerant smile as he glanced at his watch, whilst giving answer.

'Yes, indeed so. The Belle des Ames; the 'Mother of the Souls'. That is one who *cares* for people.'

'She sounds nice,' whispered Hannah, all but to herself. 'You're fond of her, Sir?,' she also whispered by way of a question.

The Knight smiled softly.

'Yes. She saved my life some time ago. The Doctors were at a loss, Mother JuJu was not. A single night of her administrations and, hey presto!, I was well again.'

Sir John had spoken lightly on the matter, but it was clear the event had been anything but.

Hannah had a strange sense of something when asking her next question.

'Where did she come *from*, John: to be with you, help you, I mean?'

'America, Hannah,' answered the Knight in a matter-of-fact way, although he had been surprised by the question. A knowledge behind it, perhaps?

'And what about this Bois Cainman?,' asked Hannah, in a more playful mood.

'Well,' responded the Ambassador, 'as stated, it's supposedly the Voodoo heart of the Island. We hear there is a fire-dancer there claiming to be the true JuJu; magic man and priest. Also, that he's a direct descendent of Boukeman, who led the slave revolt in the seventeen hundreds. Possibly so, but then most of the male natives claim such descent. If all were taken at their word, Boukeman would have sired a regiment at least!'

'But you like the people, Sir John,' suggested Hannah, by way of an indirect statement.

'Yes, child. Greatly so,' the Ambassador confirmed, with a particular gravitas.

Hannah smiled gently. It was good. Sir John clarified.

'In the main, Miss Hannah, they are a good, proud and wonderful people, on a beautiful piece of God's own land. They're honest, friendly, and much abused over the years; by their own, as well as by foreigners.'

There was another question on Hannah's lips, which she just had to ask.

'Do you believe, Sir John? Do you believe in ... in ...?'

She was unable to complete her question, trailing off meekly.

'Plura In Caelo et Orbe Terrarum, my dear', spoke the Knight, by way of extricating his host from her own predicament, and concluded, sans any dramatic emphasis, with Shakespeare's take on such matters. 'There are more things in heaven and earth ...' He did not complete the Hamlet quote.

A moment of pause, then Sir John spoke again, quite surprising Hannah with *his* question.

'Do you mind me escorting you this night, Hannah?'

'Oh, no!,' exclaimed Hannah. 'I've never been escorted by a real live Knight before!'

Sir John burst out laughing.

'Oh, very good. The 'alive' bit, I mean!'

Hannah also burst out laughing. She liked this so very, very English of Englishman, but his question did still puzzle her. The Knight gave an unsolicited answer.

'I'm glad, as I do not wish to impose. You know, your Joe does tend to want control of everything.'

Hannah smiled, as she did know, all too well. Even so, she had a question.

'But you, sir, a Knight of the Realm and an Ambassador. Bit cheeky, really.'

Sir John thought for a moment.

'Not really, dear. We had a few drinks together, your Joe and I. He told me of this planned visit. Hoped he wouldn't get delayed, but that if he did ...'

The Knight trailed off, then concluded.

'Excellent forward planning, what?'

Both laughed.

Then came the knocking at the door. Hannah got up from the bed, moving to answer, as Sir John seemed to rise from his chair with effortless, manly grace, then stood ramrod straight, eyes firmly set towards the door, ready to greet the caller.

Mamma Belle, Belle des Ames; the 'Mother of the Souls' had arrived. By another title, the 'Mother JuJu'.

Closer now the time.

Suddenly, for just a few moments, Hannah felt apprehensive and stood back, motioning for her Knight, sans his shining armour, to fill the breach. He did so, stepping forward briskly and opening the door like a butler to the manner born.

As the Ambassador stepped back and slightly to one side, it allowed Mamma Belle to sweep regally into the small suite.

To himself alone, a private thought within Sir John: *now* the two; in the one place, the one country.

The new arrival was a large lady, yet like to many of such size, she had a beautiful, fluid grace of movement. And this lady also possessed an aura and presence about her that was magical, tangible and fully equal to her frame and fame. In dress, she might have just come from the races. A large, red cotton dress, covered in multi-coloured floral design, with a wide-brimmed hat to match. She also had a rather large, pink shoulder bag that she tended to cling to. She was Mulatto; of black and white parentage. Her skin was a pale brown and without blemish. She had a large, wonderful smile and, most remarkable of all, the largest, most beautiful of deepest blue eyes. Truly, this 'Mother of the Souls' was a sight to behold.

As Sir John quietly closed the door, 'Mamma Belle', as she preferred her friends to call her, looked on at Hannah, as she herself gazed in awe at the new arrival. All apprehension left her. She *knew* this wonderful woman, but did not know how or when she might have seen her before. Memory had she none. And yet she felt a part of her, and it was beautiful.

Mamma Belle moved to the young lady, arms outstretched. As she had spoken, Mamma had taken Hannah's hands in hers as she radiated the most wondrous and loving of smiles. Hannah simply bathed in the unfolding warmth. Sir John watched silently on as Mamma worked her magic.

Mamma Belle's voice itself would prove remarkably light and melodious, the words lyrical.

Sir John made the introductions.

'Mamma Belle, this is Miss Hannah Carr. Miss Hannah Carr, this is *the*, *our* 'Belle des Ames', Mother of the Souls' … including ours!' 'Mamma Belle' to all who know and love her.'

'Hello, Hannah. A lovely name for a lovely child,' announced Mamma Belle, in a gentle manner.

The sentiments expressed might have seemed a little condescending, too familiar by far, especially from a stranger. However, Hannah did not see it that way at all, and Mamma knew it wasn't so. No stranger was she. For Hannah, from the first moment of their meeting, was grateful for it, and she *did* feel like a child in such a presence. Also, slightly vulnerable before such an undoubted power.

Sir John stepped in closer to the ladies, as he addressed himself to the new arrival.

'Mamma Belle, I'm escorting this delightful young lady to the Bois Cainman this evening. Her young man arranged it, but he's been delayed in London by a few days, so asked if I'd attend her.'

Mamma frowned for just a moment, whispering a reply, without taking her eyes of Hannah, whom she still held close.

'So soon?'

'You've heard something, Mamma Belle?', queried Sir John.

This time, Mamma turned towards the Ambassador as she gave answer, shrugging her shoulders as she did so.

'So-so'.

She then addressed herself directly to Hannah.

'Miss Hannah, would you oblige an old woman's whim and allow me to join you and Sir Johnny tonight?'

The question was lightly put, but held an earnest request.

Hannah felt as though something was happening, a pattern forming, events falling into place, into alignment, the necessary principal characters present. She still, nonetheless, looked to Sir John for guidance. He in turn smiled at her, nodding in the affirmative.

'Oh, yes please, Mamma Belle,' answered Hannah in genuine gratitude, although not quite knowing why.

Mamma smiled her thanks, knowing exactly why. Then, in an instant, without thought and in the most natural way, Hannah flung her arms around the lady's neck.

'Ah, bless, child, bless,' responded Mamma, holding Hannah close, and her shoulder bag equally close!

Then, in an iota of cosmic time, Mamma Belle realised the truth of it: She had been right when first they met. This truly was *the* child.

Sir John made an observation, in a playfully mocking way.

'I don't think she believes in the old magic, Mamma Belle.'

Mamma Belle gently moved Hannah just a slight distance from her, looking and frowning at her. She then, ever so gently, stroked Hannah's left cheek with the back of her right hand, whispering as she did so.

'As you truly believe in the Lord Jesus Christ, as I know you do sweet child, believe.'

Suddenly, as if at the flick of a switch, Belle was once more laughter and light, with Sir John immediately responding in kind. He tapped his watch.

'I think it's time for you and I to depart, Mamma Belle,' the Knight suggested.

As the Ambassador moved towards the door, Hannah grabbed her keys from the bedside table, then moved to and linked her arm into Belle's, declaring as she did so, that she'd see them on their way. In another moment, all three were bound for the lift.

Mamma smiled as they made their way, putting a question to Hannah.

'Is your beau a nice young man, child?'

'Oh yes, Mamma, absolutely so!,' answered Hannah most surely.

'That's good, then,' replied Mamma Belle, giving out with a great laugh.

Mamma then put another question as they journeyed down in the lift and into the hotel lobby.

'You gonna have kids, Hannah?'

'Most surely shall,' responded Hannah, laughing as she did so. 'Lots!'

As the little party moved towards the revolving doors and so out of the hotel, Hannah found herself turning from thoughts to the future, to thoughts immediate. Things were happening, both to her and around her. Also, in a way she could not articulate, she was *changing*, growing stronger – in the mind.

'You seem to have found yourself a new friend, Hannah, and you a kindred spirit, Mamma Belle,' observed the Ambassador, fracturing Hannah's thoughts.

Mamma gave a deep-throated chuckle as she answered, looking at Hannah as they all paused at the revolving doors.

'I think we found each other, Sir Johnny. Hey, honeychild?'

Hannah smiled at the question Mamma Belle had addressed to her directly. Inside, her soul silently wept, seemingly without reason.

Once out of the hotel and into the sunlight, Hannah's darker thoughts slipped into the shadows.

It was time for temporary goodbyes.

Hannah smiled and even managed a laugh as she hugged *her* new friend, with Sir John standing just behind them. She was also not slow to note that Mamma still clung to her shoulder bag.

Something else.

From the moment all three had left the lift and stepped into the well-appointed lobby, Hannah had reason to believe that Mamma Belle was somewhat more than she presented herself to be. Most, Islanders especially, looked towards her, totally ignoring Hannah and Sir John. Most smiled, seemingly genuinely pleased to see the lady, but others appeared to stand back, a certain apprehension in their manner.

It had also been quite obvious that the hotel staff knew Mamma Belle well, paying much deference towards her. For her part, she treated them all the same, with a mixture of politeness, charm and good nature.

And then, a car pulled silently up to the hotel entrance, stopping directly alongside Mamma Belle and her small party of two. The passenger door was opened by a hotel attendant, who then gestured, in deference, for Mamma to take her place in the plush, well-upholstered back seat. It was a wondrous sight to behold, as the automobile was a 1957 Cadillac: big and PINK! It was perfectly complemented by a tall, handsome male Islander in full chauffeur regalia – also PINK, right down to the knee-length, pink leather boots!

Hannah had first gasped and then shrieked in sheer joy at the sight before her, as she clapped her hands in delight. For her part, Mamma Belle also laughed as she expressed her joy at Hannah's obvious delight. Sir John had simply stood back, looking benignly on. He'd seen it all before.

'Forgive me, child,' spoke Mamma Belle to Hannah, 'one of my little weaknesses. I like some vroom-vroom in my life.'

Hannah laughed aloud once more and did what she believed to be the most natural of things. Once more she flung her arms around the big woman's neck and hugged her. Mamma reciprocated in kind, clinging on to her shoulder bag and calling out as she did so.

'What about this English reserve we keep hearing about, Sir Johnny!?'

Sir John just smiled as he stood by the open passenger door, waiting for the ladies to disengage themselves. The chauffeur just smiled as he got back behind the wheel.

The ladies disengaged, and Mamma negotiated getting into the back of the car, even it not being as big as she would have liked. Once safely seated, Sir John got in beside her. Before he closed the passenger door, he called to Hannah.

'We'll be here for you at eleven, Hannah. Be ready, as we'll be leaving immediately. It's a long drive.'

Hannah acknowledged the instruction and waved goodbye as the car glided silently and majestically away.

As she returned to her suite, she was deep in thought, trying to remember what had made her momentarily sad, before whatever it was had departed her mind. Something she had not forgotten, although she had thoroughly enjoyed the experience, was how everything seemed to have been staged, choreographed, from the moment Sir John had first made his appearance. It had been a performance le grande, with the Belle des Ames being the Diva. But who then the audience, and for why? Was it just for Hannah, and for what reason, if any? And where did her beloved Joseph fit into it all?

Whatever answers there might be, Hannah found herself strangely at peace. Quite calm and in control of her situation. In fact, she had never felt so safe in her young life, nor so strong in mind. Someone, or some*thing* was watching over her, and the night was far from over; as yet, not even truly begun.

At some point, for but a moment, a revelation came to Hannah. Mamma Belle was dying – of cancer. At the moment of the knowing, it had evaporated from her memory.

In the car, Mamma Belle and Sir John rested in the long and ample pink leather back seat.

'You think something will happen tonight?,' queried Sir John calmly.

'Perhaps,' Mamma answered, in some vague, seemingly far away manner. 'I heard rumours, and time ain't on our side, honey. Sweet Jesus, it ain't. Anyway, I don't think I honour our culture enough. Too blasé about it, being on our own doorstep an' all'.

Belle's humour picked up a little, but even Sir John felt just a little uncomfortable. Somehow, events seemed just a little too pat, the scenario a little too much by design; but by whom? For all that, he trusted his friend of some years standing, and without reserve.

Mamma Belle spoke, breaking into Sir John's thoughts.

'And you, Sir Johnny?,' queried the woman of true, Light magic . 'What about you?'

'As said, dear lady, reminded Sir John. 'I promised Joseph last year. Odd how things happen.'

Mamma Belle, looking away from the Ambassador and much loved friend, smiled to herself as she gave answer.

'True enough.'

Sir John eyed his companion of the hour slyly.

'Is there something you're not telling me, Belle?'

'No, darlin', was the good humoured reply. 'But, Bois Cainman ain't going to be no Ascot, that's for sure!'

Both laughed. The chauffeur did not. Indeed, Sir John knew KuJu, for that was the man's singular name, was more than just a chauffeur. He was also Mamma Belle's bodyguard and confidante, and the Ambassador's friend also.

'What time do you want picking up, Sir Johnny?,' Mamma asked.

'That's very sweet of you, Mamma, but there's no need to go out of your way.'

'I won't be, honey', was the lady's immediate riposte. 'He's driving,' she clarified, patting KuJu's shoulder as she laughed, with him joining in.

'Besides which,' added Mamma, 'you're still our guest, Mamma Queenie Lizzie's Ambassador or no!'

'Sir John gave acknowledgement with an appreciative nod of the head, whilst Mamma gave a gloriously full-throated laugh.

'My residence, say ten-thirty?'

'You got that, KuJu?,' called out the lady.

'No problem, Mamma Belle,' called back KuJu, laughing.

'That's settled, then,' responded the Ambassador. 'I'll call Hannah when I get home and confirm the timings.'

'And then we shall see what we shall see,' spoke Belle, the Mere des Ames. She added a softly spoken request, almost after an afterthought. 'And, my dearest of all Knights, please humour me this night and bring your bang-bang along.'

Although Mamma Belle's words held humour, and accompanied by a smile on her face, the request was all too serious.

'Necessary? For Hannah's sake?,' asked Sir John, even as the car was glided to a halt outside his official residence.

'Yes, and no,' answered Mamma Belle, and then clarified. 'Possible danger for us, Sir Johnny, but nothing above, on or in the depths of Hell itself shall harm that child; not this night nor any night whilst I live.'

The declaration had been made with a mix of sadness as well as defiance. Also, what Mamma knew, no one else did. Latent deep within her, Hannah was possessed of a power far, far greater than even Mamma Belle's, but would not be revealed any time soon.

It was done. Sir John alighted from the magnificent car and, as he closed the passenger door, he smiled at Mamma Belle as he patted his left jacket pocket, speaking as he did so.

'Fear not, good lady, I never travel without my bang-bang.'

Even spoken in jest, there was an edge and purpose to his words. For her part, the Belle des Ames rested back in her seat, as she signalled KuJu to drive on. In moments the car was out of sight. Only the business of the night remained.

Fire

The hour had arrived. Hannah found it a little surprising as regards to how she felt. A mix of excitement, eagerness and expectancy. In a way, she felt more like a schoolgirl on her first trip abroad, rather than a relatively experienced traveller. Maybe it also had something to do with the company in which she now found herself, and *where* she was going, and to *what?*

So came the eleventh hour of the evening, and with it, her new companions. As Hannah entered the car, there was Mamma Belle, dressed in a long, flowing, black cotton dress, and her mood strangely subdued, and still in possession of her shoulder bag; only this one was black. Subdued or no, Mamma Belle was as warm and gracious to Hannah as she had been at their first meeting.

Hannah thought upon that. Perhaps Mamma wasn't feeling up to the evening. Perhaps she knew too much concerning what Hannah would witness for the first, and probably not the last time.

The reality was that Mamma Belle was not so much in the car as on an altogether different plane, where only the JuJu could or would want to be. ***Le Diable de Feux*** would be at the fire this night, so Mamma JuJu had learnt. But for whom?

At a much, much later time, Hannah would describe the location they were driven to as being a cross between a jungle bivouac and an American Summer Camp. There was a charge in the air. A frisson. Much expectancy.

And then there was KuJu, seemingly more evident in his presence, positive in his manner. He was, this night, totally Mamma Belle's confidante and bodyguard. He also seemed to be keeping an eye out for Hannah. In every respect, he was en garde. As for the Knight, Sir John also appeared sober in his manner and, for the first time since Hannah could recall since meeting him, keeping one hand in the left pocket of his jacket. Seeing this had made Hannah look to Mamma Belle. Sure enough, she still had a firm hold of her shoulder bag.

Above and beyond all of this, there were Mamma Belle's large, deepest of blue eyes. This night they had a rather distant look within them. It made Hannah want to comment on such to Sir John. He saw in an instant and, pursing his lips, made a soft "Sssshh" sound, whilst at the same time giving a reassuring smile.

When the small party arrived at the venue, the four were led through the already seated throng about the great pit of fire, itself some thirty feet in length and fifteen feet in width. On the far side of it, a form of stage, more like a conventional platform, constructed of tar-treated, roughly hewn planks of wood. The purpose of its existence would soon be made clear.

The small party settled themselves on the ground at the very front and to the centre. Hannah was much aware that all eyes seemed to be on them, the more so on both her and Mamma Belle, with a mix of fear, awe, respect and ... *fear*? KuJu was to the left of his Mamma JuJu, Hannah immediately to her right, with Sir John immediately to her right. At Mamma Belle's instruction, they all interlinked arms.

As they settled in their positions and Kuju looked on at the dim glow of the pit embers, his Belle des Ames had squeezed his right arm. For his part, Sir John had a strong feeling that the fire dancing would prove only to be prelude to the main event.

Mamma Belle turned to Hannah, squeezed her arm and whispered words: such words, and which only Hannah would hear.

'Don't fear none, child, for nothing shall harm thee this night. Mamma des Ames says it so.'

At the time, Hannah did not understand the reasoning behind the declaration, but at the moment of the saying, she felt totally invulnerable.

The Ambassador, unaware of what had just taken place, made his own small contribution by gently, patting Hannah's right hand, accompanied by a reassuring smile. He then reassured himself by discreetly patting the pocket on the left side of his jacket. He also harboured thought on the fact that if the item were not sufficient to the need, there was also the item in Mamma JuJu's shoulder bag, should it prove necessary.

Suddenly, an explosion of action, noise and colour, a pounding of drums, as from the left and right, onto the makeshift stage on the far side of the pit from Mamma Belle and her party, leapt some thirty bare-breasted native women, clad only in long straw skirts. The thing that captivated were the lights that swirled all about and around; over their heads, around their torsos and between their legs. Slowly, the closer onlookers were able to grasp the exact nature of the dancing lights. Each dancer had, in both hands, long golden threads, on the end of which were small glass spheres, in which appeared to be tiny lighted candles. Even as the women danced, the embers in the great pit began to glow brighter, accompanied by a greater heat.

The sky above was deepest black, no stars nor clouds to behold. The drums beat faster, the heat and humidity of the night, the dancing, whirling women and the swirling lights providing a heady mix. Hannah was entranced, Sir John enjoyed the reprise of such evenings past, whilst KuJu simply observed from a mental distance. As for Mamma JuJu, she sensed she was not alone. That another JuJu of almost equal power was close to hand. Yet, whenever Hannah squeezed her arm, Belle betrayed nothing, but simply responded in kind, and displayed that wonderful smile.

And so the dance and drums continued on.

More frantic now the dancing, faster, higher and more swirling the lights, like countless, fiery sprites of the night. And the drums. *Those drums!* Faster, louder, pounding drums. And then there was the pit, Hell's own fireside; the embers ever brighter, glowing red, the heat hotter yet.

Of one thing, Hannah had not given a thought. She was totally unable to spy out the drummers and their drums.

How long the dancing went on was hard to tell, so entranced and in the moment were all present. Be that so, it came to its close in a spectacular crescendo, and in a trice the dancers were gone, the drums silent, the night once more silent and still.

Everyone waited. The embers of the pit glowed ever more fiery, red and gold. A wind seemed to spring up from nowhere. Hannah remained entranced. Sir John was realising this night was somewhat different from those past that he had attended. Mamma Belle and KuJu remained en garde.

And then it happened. From the far right-hand corner of the pit, striding out from the darkness, he, *It* came.

'Le Diable de Feux!!'

'The Demon of the Fire!,' Mamma Belle had cried out, and so it was. The second most powerful JuJu present that night. And it sought to destroy a true and rare *white* JuJu, and successor-elect to the 'Belle des Ames', the 'Mother of the Souls': **Hannah Carr**.

The speed, fluidity and restrained power with which Mamma Belle disengaged herself from Hannah and sprung to her feet was astounding, matched only by KuJu, as they both made to confront the crazed thing that came leaping out from the pit, not towards the Mamma Belle, but to Hannah.

People screamed as the demon made great strides through the fire, out from the pit and directly to Hannah. The tall, black, skeletal creature seemed to be all but flying now. What followed next, to Hannah, was if in some dream, or nightmare, which she fully played her part.

At the last, the demon, in human form, eyes fire-filled, changed direction just slightly, away from Hannah and directly towards the Mamma Belle; its Master's eternal enemy, a JuJu of the Light, the Meres des Ames.

In those fleeting moments, seemingly caught in fragmented time, Mamma Belle turned her upper torso just slightly, as she reached into her shoulder bag, grasped a handful of something and turned again to face the monstrosity now confronting her. Just before *It* was upon her, Hannah had risen and thrown herself at Hell's own creation, whilst doing everything she could to strike it with her clenched fists, in defence of her dark sister JuJu.

Mamma Belle had found her mark, just as KuJu was stepping between Hannah and the night's hideous creature.

The something Mamma had thrown was some consecrated earth of the Island. Its own carpet, on which its children did walk, work, play and simply live. It had hit the thing fully in its grotesque face.

In another moment, it had screamed a scream powerful enough to awaken the dead, lashed out, and in a prodigious leap, had cleared the heads of all before it and fled into the darkness of the night from whence it had come. Shots rang out, as Sir John gave chase, firing his revolver, with KuJu close behind him.

Pandemonium now reigned. The Islanders in the audience believed what they had witnessed and could not flee fast enough. Others, who believed it to be a somewhat unexpected part of the act, but even so, were feared enough. Three present knew all well enough. One had been protected from the truth of it all.

Mamma JuJu called aloud, strong and clear. All heard. She was summoning immediate return of her would-be protectors.

'KuJu! Johnny! Here!! We must safeguard this child above all others.'

As she had called out, Mamma had gathered a swooning Hannah, holding her, as if a babe in powerful arms.

As KuJu and Sir John returned to Mamma's side, she spoke again.

'We've got to get back to the hotel now, gentlemen, and I mean NOW!! '

KuJu and Sir John aided Mamma Belle and her charge back to their car, almost oblivious to the bedlam they left behind them.

What had transpired had been but a prelude for what was to follow. Before the night was done, another, more powerful demon would return to claim and consume the *white* JuJu.

Water

The small party arrived back at the hotel, with KuJu now having the stricken Hannah in his arms. Soon they were back in her small suite, Mamma Belle in charge of all, having discarded her black shoulder bag, knowing far greater JuJu would be needed in the hours to follow.

As Sir John stood to one side, Belle and KuJu went about their business, with barely a word spoken.

KuJu placed Hannah gently on top of the bed, then moved away to allow Mamma Belle access. She in turn looked intently at her young friend, the *Chosen One*. She was physically unharmed, but in a very deep sleep. Mamma JuJu had to reach her, so placed her hands about Hannah's head and began muttering things under her breath.

'Dans le bras desa anges, domi mon enfant.'

Whilst Mamma JuJu worked her Light magic, KuJu had attended to more earthly matters. He'd turned on the bedside light and turned off the main light, then gone over to and opened the large bay windows over to the left side of the bed. They led out to a small balcony, that itself had a small flight of steps that led straight down to the beach at the back of the hotel. After this, KuJu placed one chair in a corner close to the bed, but hidden in shadow. He then went to Sir John, holding out his hand and smiling, as a tolerant father might request a son to give attendance. The Ambassador seemed to know instinctively what he had to do. He removed his old service revolver from his jacket pocket and handed it to KuJu, who briefly gave reason.

'As long as *It* doesn't see a threat from you, Sir Johnny, you're safe. This way, if you please.'

With that request, KuJu took Sir John by the arm and gently steered him towards the chair he had placed in a corner to the bed and opposite to the bay windows. He eased the Ambassador down into the chair, whispering a parting instruction as he did so.

'Be still and silent, Sir Johnny, and no harm will befall you.'

With that said, to be on the safe side, KuJu passed his right hand across Sir John's face, so sending the man into an instant state of sleep.

With Sir John taken care of, KuJu joined Mamma Belle at Hannah's bedside.

'See how she fought for her sister, KuJu?', whispered the Mamma in excitement and great pride.

Her next words, albeit softly whispered, were hissed through clenched teeth, boding ill for someone, some *thing*.

'The bastard seeks my sister, but not for long!. I need something, KuJu, something to protect her with, to send the Devil's bastard back from whence it came.'

Brief silence, then a gasp from Mamma.

'KuJu, it's staring me in the face! Look!'

As she had spoken, Mamma Belle reached out to the thin gold chain about Hannah's long, pale, swan-like neck and, far more importantly, to the small pendant upon it, which rested at the base of the young woman's throat. A small, golden *fish*. The sign of Aquarius. **Water!**

'We have him, KuJu, we have him!,' explained the Mamma. 'Now I can my sister protect, and destroy him; *It*! A chair at the bottom of this bed, KuJu, facing the windows,' instructed Mamma Belle.

KuJu looked to his JuJu, somewhat confused, then smiled broadly as he carried out her instructions regarding a chair. She also smiled at KuJu, realising he had cottoned on to what was afoot. To be sure, she explained.

'Simple, darlin'. *It*, in whatever form, is born of fire, moves in fire, *survives* in fire, LIVES in fire. *Its* Master is the fire; the Devil Incarnate. Quench that fire, and *It* dies.'

KuJu fully understood her words, as he watched his Mamma Belle worked further, greater magic of the Light. But he also knew full well, it was costing her dearly, and that cost would be greater still. When the protection for the woman child, her sister JuJu-in-waiting, was in place, Mamma Belle leant forward, gently kissed Hannah's forehead, then stood up from the bed and moved away. Silent tears rolled down her cheeks. KuJu also wept, but within his soul, full well knowing the price his beloved Mamma could well pay.

Mamma Belle moved silently over to the Ambassador. Most probably in a loving act of farewell, she stroked his cheek and lightly kissed his forehead. A mute goodbye to one already protected in the shield of Light's own sleep, courtesy of KuJu.

Mamma Belle then stood up straight and slowly made her way to the chair KuJu had placed at the foot of the bed, speaking as she did so.

'*It's* close, KuJu.'

The night was darkest dark, still, oppressively humid, as Mamma JuJu summoned up the element within her mind. Shortly, it would answer the call, join its sister, the sea, to confront the Devil's own.

Now all had become enfolded in a gentle breeze, itself wrapped in silence. A calm before the storm – of fire.

Hannah was now in the realm of water. Warm, cascading, soothing, diamond-shimmering water. As a sight, it was beautiful. As a shield it was impregnable. Hannah felt warm, safe and *dry*. Also, possessed of an unspoken knowledge that no one, no *thing*, from any time, place or dimension, neither Man nor demon could reach her. Mamma had made it so. Her life was the child's ultimate shield.

As KuJu now stood silent behind the seated Mamma Belle, she spoke once more.

'The hour is at hand, KuJu. When the Demon of the Fire is upon us, air, wind and their sister, water, shall bind as one, and as one, evaporate and vanquish Hell's own, casting it back from whence *It* came.'

And then *It* was there, leaping through the open bay windows: The Demon of the Fire. The single blessing being that *It* was not *the* Devil itself from the pit, so not totally omnipotent. Its haste had made it blind to something at least its equal in power. At the foot of the bed, even as it made to strike at the 'child', *It* suddenly realised that something was wrong. In the muted light lay its own demise.

From the darkness, KuJu beheld the fearsome sight. It stood some eight feet tall, with a red-raw skeletal frame and barely human of shape. Wisps of smoke emitted from its form, eyes and mouth aflame. *It* that had been spewed from the pit, now ever more fearsome in its countenance.

And then it struck, throwing back its head and letting forth an unearthly cry, casting its head forward, so sending searing tongues of flames towards Hannah, herself oblivious to all. The flames never reached her. Something unseen drenched them, extinguished them. The Demon's cries of anguish and frustration rang out as red-hot steam fast filled the room, yet nothing touched.

Again, the Demon struck. This time *It* sent forth thousands of tiny, flickering tongues of flame. Yet again, the unseen element drenched them, extinguished them. As fast as the Demon could send forth the sprites of fire, so they evaporated in multiple puffs of steam.

For Hannah, her dream became ever more beautiful, fanciful and … *magical*.

Hundreds upon hundreds of tiny sprites of fire, licks of flame, darting and leaping to and fro, hurtling themselves at the cascading, diamond-shimmering water that shielded the deeply comatose young woman. Her face reflected the joy and wonderment of a child.

Now Mamma JuJu brought forth the wind. It came and swirled all about the Demon, holding it fast, as *It* itself became enfolded in a horror of its own making. The flames it had issued forth had to be satisfied, be fed. If such were not to be so, they would turn upon their own creator and consume *It* whole.

The suite was now filled with a sickening, cloying, acrid stench, and an almost unbearable heat. Even so, nothing seemed to reach out and damage the fabric of the room, nor the occupants therein. It was now time to end it all.

As Hannah "saw" the tiny tongues of flames fading, the Demon of the fire screamed aloud at what it beheld. *It* was no longer master of the hosts, but falling victim to them; they would not be denied. They had to feast before returning from whence they had been summoned: Hell's own fire.

The red, fiery flicks of flame turned deep blue, came together as one, surged forward and engulfed their 'father' Demon, and *It* itself began to burn. For just a moment, all was a sheet of blue flame, at its heart therein, gigantic in proportion, a pair of great, so deeply blue, blazing eyes.

In this time, the Belle des Ames, Mother of the Souls, final act, even as the Demon was being consumed by its own children took place. At the moment of its last scream, from a soul condemned millenniums past, with two spears of blue flame rushing out from the vacated eye sockets, where once two slits of fire had resided, a vast wave from some other place crashed down and swept Hell's own from the suite.

With the passing of the Demon, so evaporated the smoke, the steam and foul stench. The suite and its occupants therein safe, untouched, as though *It* had never been present, no conflict taken place.

Silence. All was silence. Stillness and calm. The lightest of cool breezes now filled the suite. It was done.

KuJu stepped from behind Mamma Belle's chair and turned on one of the brighter table lights. His face was bathed in sweat, his eyes betraying what he had beheld, and now the tragedy it had left in its wake. Silently, he bent over his beloved Mamma JuJu, feeling for her pulse at wrist and neck. He bent lower to look closely at the bowed head, then put his ear to the Mamma's mouth as she uttered seemingly inaudible words. KuJu appeared to repeat them in a whisper as he slowly stood upright before the chair, looked upwards to the heavens and proclaimed aloud her plea:

'Dans votre soin, Jesus doux, je recommande mon spirit.'
(*'Into Thy care, sweet Jesus, I commend my spirit'*)

'The last words spoken by my Mamma JuJu,' explained KuJu, to those still unconscious, beyond the hearing.

A few more moments of Stillness, then KuJu did what had to be done.

He went first to the house 'phone on the bedside table, made a quick internal call, then replaced the receiver. He then bent over Hannah, touching her forehead and blowing gently on her mouth, speaking words as he did so.

'Reveille-toi mon enfant parce less jours sont a toi.'
(*'Awaken child, for the days are yours'.*)

KuJu then made his way over to the Ambassador, flicking the fingers of his left hand in front of Sir John's face, whilst making a passing motion across the Knight's face with his right hand. He then stood back, speaking soft words as he did so.

'Ill east Fait'.

(*'It is done'.*)

Sir John was fully awake almost in an instant. He blinked a few times as he saw KuJu standing before him. Taking the man's arm, KuJu assisted the Ambassador out of the chair.

In actuality, physically, Sir John was fine, feeling quite strong and reasonably steady. It was his thinking processes that were a little awry.

The Knight looked across the room, seeing Mamma Belle's slumped form in the chair. He then looked to KuJu, speaking his question in look alone, with the latter nodding in the affirmative.

'Yes, Sir Johnny, it is done. Mamma Belle has given to us "Mamma Hannah" this night.'

Sir John grasped both KuJu's arms in a fleeting moment of joy and understanding at what had just been said, then looked past his friend towards Hannah, who was now stirring on the bed, slowly pushing herself up into the sitting position.

Sir John knew the folklore well enough, but to be witness to its reality, if only partially!

With his mind clearing, his thoughts became a little more ordered, the Ambassador slowly made his way over to the young lady on the bed, now fully herself the 'Mother of the Souls'. As he approached her, looking on in wonderment, and not without a little apprehension, he beheld the gently smiling, radiant face and those very large, stunningly deepest of blue eyes that were, but a short time before, hazel in colour. And now, within them, also all the care and caring for the world. Within, the Knight wept silently, as with this "birth", had passed the life of a very dear, long standing friend: Mamma Belle.

Whilst the Ambassador had moved to pay honour to the new Meres des Ames, KuJu had made his way back to the slumped and silent figure in the chair and knelt in silent prayer, devoutly wishing for the safe deliverance of the great soul into the care of the ancestors of them both.

More silent moments passed as KuJu prepared himself for what he next had to do, and it would not, for him, be easy. The passing on of the one, the arrival and acceptance of another.

By now, Hannah had risen silently and gracefully from the bed, and was standing directly in front of the tired, exhausted, yet mutely happy Knight. Hannah sensed and *understood* his myriad of emotions. As Mamma Belle had done, Hannah gently cupped her hands about Sir John's face, pulled his head gently forward and downwards, then kissed his forehead. The Ambassador had then taken Hannah's right hand and kissed the back of it, in an ages old act of chivalry.

'You fully understand, child?,' questioned the Knight in gentle whisper.

The new Mamma Hannah gave a silent nod of her head. What then followed was quick, all but silent and rehearsed and performed down the centuries.

Ordination of a particular kind.

KuJu lifted his hands and clapped hard, just the once. In a moment, the door to the suite opened inwards and five native Islander attendants entered. Two big, powerful men and three svelte-like young ladies. All wore long, flowing black satin robes, the ladies carrying garments and other things.

The men moved to the chair, each making the sign of the cross upon their bodies as they first beheld, then bowed before their deceased Mamma JuJu Belle. As they had done so, the three young ladies, along with Hannah, had done likewise.

As the Ambassador looked on, Hannah smiled sweetly, touching first her head and then her heart, speaking as she did so, with an assured, steady voice.

'Mamma Belle is now within me, John; my brain, my heart, my soul. We are one, hence I do not grieve.'

Even the young lady's words were now more adult, better selected, delivered. Hannah had matured, Mamma JuJu style.

The men had now lifted and, with solemn respect, carried the former Belle des Ames from the suite. Those remaining bowing their heads in sad farewell, save Hannah. For her, Mamma Belle had not passed over, simply moved to another place, within another life.

Suddenly, the three svelte-like young ladies seemed charged with a new energy, fresh purpose. They smiled and laughed as they went to Hannah, who herself was now laughing and smiling. KuJu closed the door as the two men and their charge departed. He then turned on the main lights in the suite and proceeded to move over to the obviously still somewhat sombre Ambassador.

All was now light, laughter and calm, sans any signs of the previous madness that had taken place.

As the young ladies went about their business, KuJu moved to Sir John's side, took his arm and gently began to guide him towards the open bay windows. The first streaks of light were in the heavens, giving notice of the imminent arrival of the new day to be.

As the two men had moved about face, the three young ladies had then given their undivided attention to Hannah, smiling and giggling as they quickly and expertly divested their new Mamma Belle of her outer clothes in a trice and slipped a plain, bright red and gold, full-length, satin garment over her head and body.

Hannah continued to give the ladies a radiant smile, accompanied by a laugh of both joy and excitement. It was a happy time. She and Mamma Belle were now one. Mourning was yet to have its hour.

KuJu and Sir John, on hearing the laughter, turned around. Both smiled. They also knew it was a time of renewal, of joy and celebration. The Transubstantiation of Hannah was complete.

KuJu was content. The orchestrator of all was satisfied. He viewed his *renewed* Mamma and would serve her equally well in the years to follow, would be Mamma Hannah JuJu's life-long chauffeur, confidante and guardian.

Now, only the closure remained. KuJu clapped his hands once more, towards the attendants, who giggled and laughed their delight, with Hannah happily doing likewise. Both KuJu and Sir John smiled, as if indulging children, but only for a few moments, as Hannah then took charge, proceeding to kiss the cheeks of each of the ladies in thanks before they scurried from the suite.

Time to do. KuJu nodded to Hannah, knowing she had already prepared herself. Once more, the remarkable, supposed simple chauffeur set about seeing to a good, kind, God-fearing man and true friend. He took the Ambassador's arm once more and gently steered the true blue English gentleman on to the balcony, thence to the small steps leading down to the soft, white sand of the beach.

As they turned to the left to make their way to the steps, Sir John looked once more into the suite, preparing to wave goodbye to Hannah. She was no longer there.

As he and KuJu set foot on the beach, Sir John felt it good to be back out and into the fresh air, blissfully unaware of the nature of the momentous event that had come to pass in that small hotel suite. Now above were stars, and a beautiful, gold and crimson canopy slowly materialising, heralding the birth of the new day, illuminating the bay. A new dawn, in more ways than one.

KuJu took the lead as the two men strolled along the deserted beach, arms interlinked, eventually stopping and seating themselves opposite to one another, at one of the many small drinking stalls scattered the length of what seemed to be a long, never-ending beach.

Time to sit awhile, perhaps reflect on matters past.

Sir John pulled out his cigarette case from the inside pocket of his jacket, offering one to KuJu, who politely declined, stating he'd had enough of fire and smoke for one day! The Ambassador lit his own cigarette, took one long pull and slowly exhaled the smoke as he sat back in his chair. Having gathered his thoughts, articulated some.

'I didn't say goodbye, KuJu,' observed the Knight sadly. 'To Mamma Belle, I mean.'

'I know,' responded KuJu sympathetically. 'Nor I. She would not have responded. She was on a totally different plane, pure JuJu. Saving the child, protecting us all.'

'Yes,' confirmed Sir John, by way of making known his understanding of it all. 'I have to say, though, I was a little hurt, inasmuch as I wasn't taken into her confidence. I mean, it was a set-up, wasn't it?'

'Yes, Sir Johnny,' confessed KuJu, giving a charming, boyish grin, but in a moment, becoming serious.

'Dear friend of mine, things to tell. Your ignorance was your defence, your shield. Mamma knew it so, therefore made it so. Had you any real knowledge whatsoever, the Demon would have sought you out long ago and killed you.' KuJu let out a long sigh, then continued. 'Anyway, Mamma was dying, she had little time or energy to spare, needed all her strength and focus. No distractions, however good a reason. Not even for you, one of her greatest friends.'

Sir John could not help but now feel himself an ungracious, ungrateful old fool, but questioned on.

'They, Mamma Belle and Hannah, didn't first meet here, did they?'

'No,' answered KuJu, direct as ever, and smiling once more. 'Last year, Mamma went on a cultural visit to Thailand. Also, seeking about to try and find someone to take her place. It was at a tourist style fire dance that Mamma first met Miss … Mamma Hannah, as now is.'

The Ambassador expressed genuine surprise.

'So, Hannah knew all along.'

'No,' corrected KuJu, patiently, 'your God bless you, Sir Johnny. Mamma Belle *sensed* it at first sight. That she, Hannah past, was also the rarest of all – a fabled *white* JuJu; a woman of the greatest form of White Light. Magic, that is. A worthy successor to Mamma Belle.'

'How could she have been so sure, KuJu?,' queried Sir John.

'She literally nursed it, thereby sensed it,' KuJu answered. 'It wasn't hard to do. We arranged for Miss Hannah as was, to be made unconscious. A faint, you know? So, Mamma was close by and went to aid the stricken white girl. It was then.'

'So, Miss Hannah, that was, had no idea at all,' concluded the Ambassador.

'Quite so,' confirmed KuJu, a slight but warm smile on his lips.

'And Joseph?,' parried Sir John.

Patient as ever, KuJu obliged his friend with more facts.

'Yes, Sir Johnny. Until the spirit of Mamma Belle entered Miss Hannah tonight, in the act of protecting her, then she knew all. As for her man, he knew and knows nothing. But that will shortly change.'

'He'll be alright, I trust?,' queried a slightly concerned Ambassador.

KuJu pushed his chair back a little as he gave a broad grin.

'Of course. We're not savages you know! When he last went to bed, his eyes were light brown. When he next awakens, they will be pale blue.'

KuJu threw back his head as he gave out with a great laugh, then leaning forward and patting the Ambassador's knee. He enjoyed funning his friend just a little. Even so, what he had said regarding Hannah's husband's eyes was all too true.

Sir John seemed just a little confused. KuJu spoke once more, in a quiet, serious way, as one who knew well of what he spoke.

'Of Joseph's eyes, I speak true. Such will be an outward sign that he is at one with Mamma Hannah. He'll know to come quickly. We shall look after him; after them both.'

A silence descended. The new day was taking a greater hold of the sky.

'And you, KuJu,' asked the Knight. 'What of you, and just exactly *who* are you!?'

Sir John gave a warm smile as he put that question, and KuJu reciprocated in kind.

'I am JuJu, my friend, but strictly second class compared to Mamma Belle, and now Miss ... Mamma Hannah JuJu. My lot is to guard such as they, and do so, gladly, with all my heart.'

'I just knew you were no ordinary fellow, my friend,' exclaimed the Knight.

KuJu rose from his chair, so the Ambassador did likewise from his.

'Nobody is ordinary, Sir Johnny,' advised KuJu in a light hearted way.

Sir John laughed quietly as the two men once more continued to stroll along the beach.

'Too young to die, relatively speaking,' observed the Ambassador.

'Who, Sir Johnny?,' queried KuJu.

'Mamma Belle,' clarified the Ambassador.

KuJu sighed and gently patted his friend on the back.

'Sir Johnny, she was ninety-five if she was a day!'

Sir John gasped, but before he could speak further of the wonderful, but departed lady, KuJu changed the subject.

'And what for you, Sir John?,' asked a concerned KuJu. 'Where to, what to do?'

'Not sure, really,' answered the Ambassador in a reflective mood, taking a possible subtle hint. 'Getting too old for all this sort of stuff. Home to England, retirement, tea on the lawn and tending roses I shouldn't wonder.'

As Sir John had spoken, Kuju had pulled the Ambassador's gun from his own pocket, handing it to the oh, so English of men.

'Then you probably won't be needing this?,' laughed KuJu, handing the weapon back to its owner.

'Good Lord,' responded Sir John, having forgotten that KuJu had taken it from him, politely, earlier on. 'Well, who knows what I shall encounter back home in a wild, overgrown, English garden!'

'Whatever you wish for yourself, great friend of Mamma Belle, KuJu shall help make it so.'

'But I'll be back in dear Old Blighty, friend of mine,' reminded Sir John.

'And we, Ambassador, Sir, are everywhere,' came back a smiling KuJu's response.

End